THE
DARK
DIDN'T
CATCH
ME

THE DARK DIDN'T CATCH ME

Crystal Thrasher

A MARGARET K. MCELDERRY BOOK

AN ALADDIN BOOK
Atheneum

Published by Atheneum
All rights reserved
Copyright © 1975 by Crystal Thrasher
Published simultaneously in Canada by
McClelland & Stewart, Ltd.
Manufactured by Fairfield Graphics, Fairfield, Pennsylvania
Designed by Harriett Barton
ISBN 0-689-70465-8
First Aladdin Edition

This book is gratefully dedicated
to the ONES who cared:
THE CHILDREN. MINE . . . YOURS . . . and THEIRS

"Aunt Cricket, don't ever apologize for loving us."

THE DARK DIDN'T CATCH ME

chapter one

Julie, Jamie, and I climbed up the tailgate of the truck and over the furniture, digging down among the barrels and boxes to find a place where the cold November wind wouldn't hit us directly and where we wouldn't be likely to bounce out. I stumbled and fell over the rolled carpet and landed with my feet up in the air.

"Straighten up, Seely, and put your skirt down," Julie said.

I tucked my legs under me and made room for her and Jamie just as the truck gave a coughing lunge and started moving unsteadily down the lane to the main road.

Jase Perry drove the old rattletrap truck. He had been at the farm since daylight, loading and unloading the things Mom wanted to take with her to Greene County.

3

The only thing he hadn't taken off the truck at least once was the big cast-iron cooking stove. He mumbled under his breath that he knew she was taking that cook stove whether anything else moved or not.

The Perrys had been neighbors to us ever since I could remember. But for a time now, they had been living down in the Indiana hills, and we hardly ever saw them. When we were younger, we had thought Jase and Dicie were our aunt and uncle. Then, one day, Julie came home crying because Floyd Perry, their oldest, had told her she wasn't his cousin. Mom explained to us the difference between friends and relations. She ended by saying, "God gave us our relations, but thank God we can pick our own friends."

I don't know if we chose the Perrys for friends or if it was just something that grew with time. At our house we didn't seem overly blessed with friends *or* relations. The Perry kids had a grandma and an Aunt Lulu, but the only relation of ours that I ever heard tell of was our Great-grandmother Curry; and she was dead.

Floyd Perry, Mom, and the baby, Robert, who was four, sat in the front seat now with Jase. Floyd folded up his long legs, his bony knees nearly under his chin, and straddled the gear shift. Mom held Robert on her lap and sat next to the window in case she got carsick from the long drive.

If Mom didn't want to go someplace but had to go anyway, she was apt to get carsick. We would stop and wait until she guessed she was able to go on.

In the first place, Mom said, Dad had bought that

house in Greene County without ever telling her a thing about it. She had thought he was just taking a load of corn in to the grain elevator and would be home before dark.

But it had been late that night when Dad got home. Mom had walked the floor and sworn up and down that Dad had been knocked on the head and robbed of all his money. Or else the team of horses had run away with him, and he was lying hurt or maybe dead somewhere between home and the granary. I think she favored the first explanation. She mentioned it the most often.

Mom had been close to crying when we heard his step on the porch. She hurried to open the door before he'd had time to reach it.

"Where on earth have you been? Are you all right? Have you still got the money?" Mom had to stop to catch her breath.

Dad said, "You didn't ask if I was hungry or if I'd had any supper, Zel. Set out a bite for me, and we'll talk while I eat." He seemed to notice then that Julie, Jamie, and I were still up. "Why aren't you kids in bed? You'll all be late for school in the morning."

Julie said, "There's no school tomorrow. It's Saturday."

"School or no—you'll not lay abed later than six o'clock; and it's near midnight right now."

Before Julie closed our bedroom door, I heard Mom say, "I hear you note the time, Rob. Now, let's hear what kept you out till this hour of the night."

Mom woke us the next morning banging the stove lids

and dragging the iron skillet and coffee pot across the top of the stove as she started breakfast. The kitchen door slammed when she went out to gather eggs, and the oven door closed with a loud whoosh after she shoved the pan of biscuits in to bake.

"Wonder why Mom is upset this early in the morning?" I said to Julie. "We're not even up yet."

Julie smiled and nudged me toward the edge of the bed. "Suppose you get up and find out what's bothering her. I'll stay here till you think it's safe to venture in to breakfast."

I got out of my nightgown and put on the same gingham dress I'd worn the day before. Just as I stepped into the hall, Jamie opened his bedroom door. His hair, dark as a buckeye bean, fell in a mass of tousled curls over his ears and down on his forehead. I knew he'd been waiting for me. I took his hand and we went to the kitchen to wash up for breakfast.

Jamie was nine and a half, a year and a half younger than me, but small and shy for his age. He and I were Mom's in-between kids. Not old enough to be treated like grownups yet, and too big to be fussed over and babied. Mom made over Robert and went out of her way to cater to his every want, trying to keep him a baby, I guess; and she fussed at Julie, telling her to grow up and act her age. Jamie and I were left alone. We were at the stage where no one seems to expect much of kids.

At the breakfast table, Dad said, "I'll load the wagon first thing in the morning and take the livestock on ahead. That gives you a week to pack. It's a small house,

Zel, so take only the things you'll need to set up house-keeping."

Mom said, "I won't step a foot out of this house. I don't know how you can expect me to just pack up and leave everything."

"Jase says I can get work down there. There's a good stand of timber on the place and money to be made cutting props and rail ties for the mines. Art Sudlow is taking the team of horses off my hands. He'll pick them up at Jase's. After I get the stock settled in the barn, I'll stay at the Perrys'. Their place is just a little ways back in the hills from your house."

"Don't call it my house," Mom said. "I want no part of it."

Dad went on talking as if Mom hadn't opened her mouth.

"Jase will be here next Saturday morning with his truck. You have things ready to go when he gets here. I'll be at the house to help Jase unload the truck and set up the stoves when you all get there."

Dad left for Greene County the next morning. He took the pigs, our pet lambs, crates of squawking chickens, and feed for the animals in the farm wagon. The cow was tied to the back of the wagon with a lead rope. She bawled and swung her head as if to say she wouldn't go either. As the wheels began to turn, she braced all four feet, and when the rope tightened, first one leg and then the other gave way and buckled under her. She stumbled, then got to her feet, and lumbered along after the wagon.

We had watched until Dad and the wagon were out

of sight. Julie had said, "It would make more sense to take the heating stove along on this first load with the animals. Then the house would be warm when we got there."

But the fat black monster with the isinglass face and cast-iron ruffle around its hips was riding here on the loaded truck with us.

Jase stayed on the back roads and bypassed all the towns. The roads had been graded and tarred sometime in the past, but now the chuckholes were deep enough to bury one of our hogs, and they lay as close together as a man's tracks. I think Jase hit nearly every one of them.

We bounced up and down on the back of the truck, scraping our knees and elbows on the rough edges of the barrels and Mom's bedsprings. It seemed like every time we got warm and comfortable, Jase would hit another chuckhole or swerve to miss one, and we would go tumbling from side to side.

Soon after we crossed the fork of White River, Jase stuck his head out the window and yelled, "You kids back there, hang on tight! You're in Greene County now."

As if that was the signal it had been waiting for, the pockmarked blacktop turned into a barely passable road of shallow gravel and frozen ruts of red clay.

Suddenly the truck seemed to stand on its nose. All the boxes shifted and slid forward making our cramped space even smaller. I caught hold of the sideboard and pulled myself up, then braced against the rail; I looked over the top. The road went straight down with a sharp bend at the foot of the hill.

Jase changed the gears, and I fell back on the carpet roll. Then as I tried to sit up, the gears clashed again, slowing the truck to a jerking near standstill. When Jase shifted the gears again, the truck groaned and shook itself like a dog after a rainstorm. I was sure it was falling apart, but it held together, and we slowed to a crawl for the sharp turn.

After we had rounded the bend, we could see that the road had many such twists and turns as it climbed to the top of another hill and meandered off through the woods, to lose itself among the trees. The truck labored and nearly stalled on the steep grades. Julie said if the back was heavier than the front, the truck would tip on end going up the steep hills. Jamie and I crept forward until we touched the cab and clung to the slat sides with both hands, adding our weight to that of the front end.

Huge trees grew near the tracks we followed through the woods. Branches and bare limbs spread across the way and threatened to sweep us off the heaped load. On one side we looked down into wooded ravines a hundred feet deep. On the other side, hills, slashed through with ragged, red-edged gullies, rose just as high. First the hill would be on one side of the road, then pretty soon it would be on the other. Whichever way Jase turned, there was always a hill and a hollow on either side of us.

The hills grew higher and the ruts in the road got deeper as we crept farther into the strange, unknown county soon to be our home. We saw a few run-down, shabby houses framed by toothless picket fences along the way. Ragged kids, followed by slat-sided hounds, ran to peek from behind trees and watch us go by. We raised our hands and called out to them, but nobody waved back at us.

Our lunch was gingersnap cookies from a brown paper sack. We didn't have anything to wash them down with, so we played a game to see who could make the most spit for swallowing them. Jamie choked on his last gingersnap, and I slapped his back until he could get his breath. His face was still purple.

Julie said, "Jamie, don't you dare have one of your spells. There isn't room in here for you to have a fit."

Jamie giggled. We wrapped a quilt around him and pulled him down between us to share our warm place.

It was nearly dusk when Jase called out the window and said, "There's your house up ahead. You're home."

The pale winter sun disappeared behind hovering dark clouds and distant hills. We could barely make out the small, weather-beaten house in the clearing.

Julie, looking at the hills surrounding us, said, "Lord, you'll have to lie on your back at high noon to ever see the sun from down here."

She was probably right. She usually was. At sixteen, Julie wasn't very big, but she knew almost everything.

I wondered what it would be like to climb to the top of the highest hill before daylight and watch the sun come out of the earth and rise to meet me. I knew it would surely be warm and sunny up there while it was still night and pitch black around this house.

Jase stopped the truck near the open-air front porch, which slumped toward the road. Its carved posts leaned forward under the weight of the tin roof, and it looked as if one step on it would bring the whole porch tumbling down upon us.

Julie and I jumped from the truck, skirted the rickety porch, and picked our way carefully through knee-high brown ragweed and many seasons of dried grass to the back door. The house looked better on the inside than it had appeared to be from the road. The room we entered ran the full width of the house with windows all along one wall and across one end. Worn blue-figured linoleum covered the area in front of the flue hole, but the rest of the floor was bare pine boards. A wide unpainted shelf was built along the wall where the stove would sit, and beneath it was a big woodbox heaped full of kindling and stove wood.

Julie waved her hand toward the shelf and woodbox. "It looks like Dad made good use of his time while he was waiting for us."

"He wasted his time if he did it for Mom. She'll see the bare floor and not even notice that it's clean."

I opened the solid oak door that separated the kitchen from a good-sized living room and one bedroom in the front part of the house. From the living room four steps led up to a small plank door; then four more steps led up to the attic. It covered the whole house and had one long narrow window at each end.

Julie and I used the brick chimney that passed through the center of the attic as a dividing line. We chose the left side next to the stairs for our bed and dresser and allowed the boys the right side for theirs.

We were tired and hungry but most of all thirsty for a drink of water. Mom said the water had to be boiled before we could drink it. No telling how long it had been since anyone had lived here. Anything could have fallen into the well. We gagged and shuddered.

Mom ordered us away from the rotten boards that covered the mouth of the well. She said it looked to be wide enough to swallow us all without leaving a trace.

"The first thing tomorrow, your dad is going to clean that well and make a decent cover for it, or I'll not stay in this godforsaken hole. And if you kids want a bed to sleep on tonight," she added, "you'll take those straw ticks out to the barn and stuff them."

We were glad for any reason to get away. The house was no place for us right then or any time when Mom felt that way.

Mom had made the straw ticks by sewing feed sacks together, leaving a slit down the center for stuffing in the straw. While Dad and Jase set up the stoves to heat the house and cook supper, we filled the ticks in the barn with clean straw for our beds.

The first night or so, the beds would be so high we'd have to take a running jump to get in, but by the end of the week the mattresses would be mashed down flat and hard on the wooden bed slats.

Only Mom and Dad had springs on their bed. And the way those wire coils screeched and brayed every time one of them turned over, I was glad we didn't have springs. Sometimes a spring would break and poke up through their feather tick. Then Dad would take the bed apart and tie the coils down with bailing wire. He would skin his knuckles and swear that bedsprings were a contraption invented by the devil to test a man's soul. But he'd fix them and wrestle them back in place before bedtime.

All the way to the barn we could hear the men cussing the stovepipes as they banged them together to get a tight fit in the flues. We stayed there in the hayloft, waiting for things to quiet down in the house.

Floyd and Julie lugged the straw-filled mattresses to the wide door of the hayloft and heaved them down to the frozen barnyard below, while Jamie and I rolled in the high straw stacks and scattered it over the loft floor. Floyd tried his best to put straw down the front of Julie's blouse, but she squealed and wiggled out of reach. Then he chased her across the loft and fell headfirst into the hay, which was stacked from the eaves to the ridgepole.

Floyd was nearly as tall as Dad and Jase but not as thick and heavy. He seemed to be all knees and elbows with a long stretch of nothing in between. Dad said Floyd was just skin and bones now, but he would be a giant when he got his growth, if he didn't stumble over his big feet and break his neck. Floyd had chipped a big piece off a front tooth, once, when he tripped and fell on the wood pile.

I was just burying Jamie under a pile of straw when I heard Mom calling us to bring the mattresses and come to supper. I dug him out and brushed away the straw as best I could. Floyd was still picking straw out of Julie's hair at the supper table.

Before they left that night, Jase said, "On Monday morning, you kids take the first mud lane you come to and follow it straight to the schoolhouse door. Come home with my young'uns. Dicie'll show you the short cut through the woods and the path across Lick Crick. Julie, you can catch the school bus with Floyd. It comes right by here."

Julie smiled at Floyd, then took a lamp and went up the attic steps to make our bed.

After Jamie and Robert had gone to sleep on their side of the attic, Julie and I put our things away and got into our outing flannel nightgowns. Before we put out the light, I turned to the stitched center of my notebook. Lines were crossed out and penciled through where I had made a mistake or changed my mind later. If I tore a sheet from the book, a clean page would fall out on the other side, so I just crossed things out.

Starting on a clean page, I wrote, "Today we traveled all the way from home to the end of the world. Dad says we will make a home here because he can find work and there is no place else to go."

Mom hollered up the steps and said, "Seely, blow out that lamp and go to sleep. You're wasting coal oil."

I turned the wick as low as it would go and still make light.

"Blow it out, I said!"

I blew; and the attic was so black I couldn't see across the room. I stuck my notebook under the straw tick, shut my eyes, and scooted up close to Julie's back.

chapter two

*J*ase came down early Sunday morning to help Dad build a platform and cover for the well. He said there was a cold mist blowing in from the east and it felt like it might snow. He didn't know if Dad would want to work on the well or not.

Mom left the room to get a warm wrap, and Dad said, "I know it's not a fit day to be working on that damn well, but if I don't get it done today, I'll never hear the last of it."

While Dad and Jase were talking over the best way to get the job done, Jamie and I grabbed our sweaters and ran outside.

The mist had turned into big wet snowflakes, which melted away as soon as they hit the ground. We lifted our faces to the snow and stuck out our tongue to catch the cold, tasteless slush in our mouth.

Before long, the snow stopped, and a cold drizzle of rain fell in its place.

Mom went to the well with Dad and Jase. "I won't know a moment's peace until that well is braced and covered."

She stood over the men, telling them what she wanted done, but finally the cold drizzle sent her back to the warmth of the kitchen. "By rights," she said, as she was leaving, "I ought to have a pump right there in the house."

Jamie and I moved closer to the well so we could watch Dad and Jase measure and cut the two-by-fours.

Dad said, "You kids stand back."

We stepped away, then crowded up close when he took the old boards off the opening to measure and fit the new cover.

"Damn it! I told you kids to get back. All your mother needs right now is to have you two young'uns fall in this well."

We sought shelter in the barn. It was dim and shadowy, with a heavy, still coldness, not the least bit like the cozy place it had seemed last night when we stuffed our mattresses.

Jamie began to rummage through an old chest full of broken harness, tools, and other farm junk. He complained it was too dark to see if anything was worth keeping. I found a lantern hanging on a peg just inside the door and a tin box of matches on the wide beam beside it. I stood on a feed box and lifted them down. Jamie said we shouldn't strike matches, but I lit the lantern, anyway, and carried it with us as we looked around the barn.

On the very bottom of the chest of old trash, Jamie found a small Indian arrowhead. He piled the junk and trash back in the chest, then searched through every corner and cubbyhole in the barn, but he didn't find another arrowhead.

I blew out the lantern and hung it back on the peg. Then we ran back to the well to show Dad Jamie's find.

While we had explored the barn, Dad and Jase had been busy. They had built an open shed over the well, shingled its roof, and laid a railing around the middle. They were nailing boards from the ground to the railing, closing in the lower half of the shed, by the time we got back.

When they heard a car drive up, Dad and Jase put their hammers down and turned to see who was coming to our house. The only man we knew in Greene County was Jase; and he was here already.

"I'll bet it's the preacher," I whispered to Jamie.

Preachers were the only people I ever saw in black suits, with hats set square across their heads. If Dad had to wear a hat, he'd tilt it a little over one eye. "Like a roving gambler," Mom said.

Jase said, real low, to Dad, "That's George Brent. On his way home from church. Wife drags him there every Sunday."

Then he raised his voice and called heartily, "Howdy, George."

The man stopped, then came on, more sure of himself

17

after seeing Jase. "Morning, Jase. Nasty weather." He turned to Dad and said, "I'm your neighbor from down the road there a-piece. Bud Watson over at the McVille general store told me he had sold this place, but I didn't expect to see the new owners moving in so soon."

Dad shook his hand, then drew his pipe and tobacco from the bib pocket of his overalls. He cupped his hands around the pipe and tamped the tobacco down with his thumb. Then he bent away from the weather to shield a match and light it. The pipe went out, but he sucked on it anyhow and fiddled with it while he talked.

"I couldn't see no reason to wait till winter was upon us to make the change. Wanted to be settled in before it turned off cold, but there's a lot to be done around here."

George said, "I see you didn't waste any time getting started on it."

"This well had to be taken care of, first thing," Dad replied. "Bad as I hate to be working on the Sabbath, it had to be done."

I thought to myself, Dad didn't have much choice in the matter. It was either displease the Lord or please Mom. And he had to live with Mom.

George had a friendly face, what we could see of it. The hat seemed to rest on his bushy black eyebrows. It shaded his eyes, and a thick black mustache drooped across his upper lip and hid his mouth. It was hard to tell if he was smiling, but he had laughter in his voice.

"Hello there, little one," he said to me. "Who is that big-eyed girl hiding behind you?"

Jamie slipped his hand in mine and tugged lightly. I held his hand and stood firm.

18

"This is Jamie," I said. "He's a brother."

Dad said, "I thought I told you kids to get in the house, out of this rain."

He didn't say it like he was angry with us for not minding him the first time, just reminding us we had no business there and should play somewhere else.

The car horn sounded in two long blasts, then a short beep-beep. George turned and waved in the general direction of the noise and called, "I'm coming, dear. I'm coming."

Then he turned his back to the road and said to Dad, "That's my wife, Clara. Good woman, but curious as a coon and impatient as a baby. Can't abide waiting."

The horn blared again, and George said, "Well, we just stopped by to see if there was anything we could do to help you folks get settled. If you need anything, give us a holler, or send one of these big-eyed young'uns down to the house to fetch us."

Dad was smiling, pleased by the offer of help from a neighbor in this strange county.

There's no doubt about Dad's smiles. They cover his whole face. His lips turn up at the corners, and deep lines crease his cheeks. Wrinkles fan out from his eyes and pucker the skin between his sandy eyebrows and high cheekbones, drawing his eyes half shut. Even his hump-backed Roman nose loses its sternness. I noticed Dad's smile was catching. Jase and George were smiling, too.

Jamie tugged at me again, urgently this time. I copied the man's voice and said, "All right, Jamie. I'm coming! I'm coming!"

The cold drizzle had changed to a steady rain by now that hit us hard when we stepped from the shelter of the covered well. We made a dash for the kitchen door.

Not much later, Dad and Jase came in soaked to the skin. Jase said to Mom that he guessed she had the only roofed wishing well in Greene County. His guess was close to the truth. Mom wished it was in the kitchen, and Dad said he wished he'd never heard of the damn thing.

It rained all Sunday night and was still sprinkling on Monday morning when we left for school. We had to be flat on our back sick and the house quarantined before we ever missed a day. I never knew for sure if they wanted us to have an education or just couldn't stand having us around underfoot.

That first day in school sticks in my mind like the red clay mud that clung to my shoes that morning and sucked them off my feet with every step I took. While I struggled to get my feet and shoes back together and take another step, I lost my balance and fell. I threw my hands out to break my fall, and both hands slapped into the clay mud up to my elbows.

Jamie, who had walked on ahead, came back and pulled me out of the mud and on to the road bank. The rain dripping from the tall weeds mixed with the tears that were running down my face.

Jamie said I looked like a mud crybaby. I laughed, then cried again when I saw the mud caked on my hands and feet and coat sleeves. He took off his cap and wiped my face and hands, then he stuck it on my head and pulled the flaps down over my ears.

"Don't cry because you got all muddy, Seely. All the other kids will be muddy, too." He smiled and added, "Unless they can fly!"

He took my hand to steady me along the slick road and held it all the way to school.

The schoolhouse was a one-room frame building that had been painted white, but the paint had cracked and washed away, leaving it a dirty, faded gray. A pencil could be dropped through the wide cracks in the board floor, and the cold wind whistled up through the openings, chilling our feet and legs. Even when I stood next to the red-hot stove in the middle of the room, my feet and legs didn't get warm.

I didn't like this school, and I didn't want to stay here with all these skinny, scrawny kids. Maybe after a while, I would shrivel up and shrink to their size, and then my eyes would be the biggest part of me, too. I cornered Jamie and whispered, "Let's go home. I don't like it here."

He shook his head, then stepped far enough away so that my whispers wouldn't reach him.

That first day, I sat at a desk in the very last row. Mr. Thompson, the teacher, said I should sit there until he could put me in my place. I thought, "That settles it." He would never be able to place me here, so he would have to send me home.

But I wouldn't leave without Jamie, I'd get him, then we would go right down that mud road, straight home. I would leave this school where no one spoke or smiled at me.

There was one tall, bony girl with dark hair hanging

straight to her shoulders from a middle part and held back from her face with a scrap of flowered gingham. She had a split place in her upper lip that looked as if it had been sewed together by a six-year-old child and had puckered.

She smiled crookedly as she moved about the room helping the little kids out of their coats and fastening or pinning their clothes together to hide their nakedness. When she spoke to them, her words slurred together, and I couldn't understand what she said. But her soft brown eyes were pretty, and I thought she looked kindly at me as she walked by.

I liked her at once. But when I smiled at her, she lowered her eyes and turned away. I didn't know what to do. Out of the two dozen or more kids in the school room, she was the only girl anyways near my size.

At midmorning, we had a twenty-minute recess. Children stood around in bunches like cows in a hailstorm, looking at Jamie and me as if they expected us to disappear into thin air. And I would have if I had known how.

Once my eyes met those of a tall boy with mussed-up red hair and clothes that looked as if he'd slept in them. I stared right back at him, daring him to speak, to say anything at all. A fight would have been better than this quiet, staring stand-off.

After recess, the teacher assigned a desk to me. "Ah, you girl," he said. "Take the seat behind Clarence," pointing to the gawky redhead who had stared so steadily at me earlier.

I couldn't see over Clarence's head, so I stared at the

back of it. "If he lived at our house, his hair wouldn't be allowed to grow that long," I thought. "Dad would cut it, if he had to take the sheepshears to do it."

When Clarence moved his head, a little gray bug scurried to the tip of his hair, fell to his shoulder and burrowed underneath his wrinkled shirt collar. His tousled hair seemed to be alive and crawling with the little bugs. I forgot the open book on my desk as I watched them and waited for each one to complete the journey from his scalp to his shirt collar.

Clarence fidgeted and scratched his head. Then he turned around in his seat and caught me staring at him.

Mom had told us and told us about staring at people.

"In the first place," she said, "it's rude. And if you stare long enough, they will turn and catch you at it."

I kept my eyes on my desk after that and pretended to read. I swore that Clarence would never again catch me looking at him; not even if he taught his bugs how to do tricks.

At last school was over. Jamie and I walked with the little Perry girls as far as their house. Dicie showed us a path, a shortcut through the woods, and gave us chocolate-covered cupcakes to eat on the way home.

"You kids stay on the path and you'll come to a foot-log across Lick Crick. Climb the bank on the other side, and you'll come out of the woods behind your barn."

We started walking slowly down the faint path through the sedge brush to the woods. Dicie called after us, "Don't poke along or stop to play, now, or the dark will catch you in the woods, for sure."

I hurried along and Jamie ran to keep up with me. At

the edge of the woods, I hesitated. The ground ahead of us was covered with leaves, and the path we were supposed to follow was hidden somewhere underneath them. Jamie stopped beside me and just stood there looking at the trees that grew tall and thick all around us.

The pale sun, which had been shining down through a hole in the clouds, slipped behind a heavier cloud and brought the dark a little closer to us.

We put off going into the woods until Jamie said, "Look, Seely. Not at the ground, but away up ahead. See how the trees part and make a road through there?"

I looked to where his hand was pointing. He was right. Up close, the ground all seemed the same, but at a distance, I could tell where the path passed through the trees.

It was twilight under the trees, and the deeper we went into the woods, the darker it got to be. The wind whistled and whined amongst the top branches. We crossed the ridge and took another bearing on our path. We were about midway down when I stepped on a patch of wet, slick leaves. My feet flew out from under me, and I slid down the muddy hill on my rump and elbows, my hands flailing thin air as they grabbed for a root or a young sapling to break my fall. Now that I needed one, the trees stood far apart and back from the path.

A rotten log lying across the way stopped my sliding, and Jamie slammed into me from behind. He grabbed me around the waist and hung on for dear life. I loosened his hands to get up. Then I saw he was crying.

"For heaven's sake, Jamie, what are you crying about? I slid down the same hill and I'm not crying."

24

He wiped at his tears with his sleeve and said, "I know you did. But you didn't come down as fast as I did."

Our slide downhill had taken us off the path and brought us to the top of a huge rock that jutted from the hillside. Patches of gray moss the size of a dishpan spotted it, and greenbriars grew in a tangled mass along one whole side.

From there, we could see a creek running between clay banks at the foot of the hill and a log wedged in place over the water for fording it.

"There's the footlog, Jamie. We're almost home."

We squatted on our heels and inched our way down the sloping side, away from the greenbriars, and jumped from the edge of the rock to the ground.

The face of the overhanging rock was nearly hidden by vine-covered trees and broken branches that lay snagged at a slant on the side of the hill. To dodge the dangling brown vines, we stepped close to the rock—and walked into a large dry space under the overhang.

I forgot Dicie's warning to hurry when I saw a cave going back into the ground. Jamie refused to go through the wide opening to the cave with me. He said it might fall in on us, even though there were layers of flat rocks packed into the dirt on either side of the cave opening, so it couldn't possibly fall. I started to go into the cave, but he grabbed my arm.

"Let's go, Seely. We'll come back some other time and bring a light with us."

"I'll bet the Indians hid in this cave, sometimes, when they used to live in these woods," I said.

Jamie moved away from me, toward the woods. "Let's

go home, Seely. For all we know, Indians may still live here."

I left the cave, and we struck off downhill in the direction of the creek. It was further away than it had looked from up there. I held onto the trees and Jamie hung onto me, as we slipped and skidded down the hill.

At the creek, we stopped and cleaned the mud and leaves off each other as best we could. Mom would probably raise Cain anyway about our muddy clothes and say we must have rolled in every mudhole we came to, to get so dirty.

Jamie crossed the footlog on his hands and knees. I looked back at the big rock to place it firmly in my mind, then dropped to my knees, and followed him across the creek.

Tree roots made steps for us to hang onto as we climbed the slick river bank on the other side. We were puffing and out of breath when we ran from the cluster of trees into a clearing and saw our barn just a little way ahead.

For just a moment before disappearing behind the hills, the sun came out of the clouds and showed its face above the tree tops.

Jamie smiled happily at me. "We're home, and the dark didn't catch us. Seely, we've outrun the dark."

chapter three

*E*very week, Mr. Thompson picked two pupils to carry the water from Old Man Bishop's well into the school. He chose me and Frieda Walters to carry water my first week there. Frieda was the girl with the harelip.

The Bishop house was empty, Frieda told me on our first day. Old Man Bishop had been dead and buried a long time, but the people down here still called it his place and his well.

"In the fall of the year," she added, "pears ripen and rot on the trees in his backyard because the kids aren't allowed to pick his pears."

"But they drink his water," I said.

"That's different," Frieda said, and didn't say anything more until we were on our way back to school with the water.

Then she shifted the bucket to her other hand and whispered, as if sharing a secret, "I don't really have to go to school. When you're sixteen, like me, you can quit any time you want to."

I was surprised she was that old, because Frieda was in the sixth grade with me. She told me that before Mr. Thompson came, the teachers didn't want to be bothered with her, because of her lisp. She finally just sat in whichever grade she had books for.

"It's mostly the slow learners who don't finish school before they're sixteen," she added.

I prayed a silent prayer that I wouldn't be a slow learner and still be in the sixth grade when I was sixteen.

Frieda hardly ever spoke in class because of her harelip, but on our way to and from Old Man Bishop's place that week she chattered like a blue jay. Friday morning, though, she seemed to be worried about something. She didn't say anything. We were crossing the playground on our way back from the well, when she asked, "Seely, do you like to carry water with me?"

I said, "Sure. Why wouldn't I? I like you. Besides, I get out of doing school work for a while each day."

She brightened up right away. Her dark eyes were shining and she looked pretty. "Let's ask the teacher if you and me can carry water all the time. We'll have to carry it when it's cold and snowing and wade through mud when it rains, but we'll get out of school work." Mr. Thompson looked surprised when we suggested it, but he agreed.

One morning as we were banging and clanging the

water buckets to Old Man Bishop's, she said, "My brother Teddy likes you. He thinks you're a cute little blond girl."

I didn't know which one was Teddy, but he must be the stupidest boy in school, I figured. Probably ugly, too, with big feet and overalls that struck him halfway to his knees, like all the other boys; and a dirty shirttail flapping out. To please Frieda, I listened when Mr. Thompson called classes up front to recite and looked at all the boys as they walked by to see which one was Teddy.

He was in the fourth grade. That was the largest class in school and took up two full rows when they recited their lessons. Everyone could get through the first three grades, but they seemed to bog down in the fourth and stay there. Each year the class grew, Frieda said, and no one seemed to mind the least bit. Some of the kids were going through for the third or fourth time.

Teddy was one of the slow learners. He was thirteen years old, and Frieda said he'd probably never get beyond fourth grade.

He was a shy, slightly built boy with dark curls that fell over his forehead, nearly hiding his solemn brown eyes. Teddy seldom smiled, but when he did, his face and eyes lit up like a freshly trimmed coal-oil lamp.

I was a homely, rough-and-tumble, towheaded tomboy, but he chose me for his best girl, anyway. After he gave me his two agate taws during the noon marble game and said I could keep them forever, the whole school knew I was his girl.

During recess, if we played hide-and-seek, Teddy let

me get home free. If I was put on the end of crack-the-whip, he ran to catch my hand and drag his feet so we wouldn't go sprawling in the dirt and dust of the playground.

For my birthday, he gave me a pen and pencil set. The pen didn't work and the pencil had been mashed on the end until lead wouldn't fit in it, but I flaunted the pen and pencil in front of the kids at school as if they were pure gold with a lifetime guarantee. But I swore Jamie to secrecy, and I never mentioned Teddy or his gift to anyone at home.

Winter came early in December and stayed. The first snow lay on the ground like a dirty white blanket and waited for fresh snow to fall and cover it. Then a blizzard, bringing more snow, froze over everything. We had to break ice on the water buckets in the kitchen to wash our face and hands before breakfast each morning.

That was a time when the fires never went out in the kitchen cook stove or the Hot Blast Florence heater in the middle of the living room floor. Dad got up in the middle of the night to lay chunks of wood on the fires to keep them going until morning.

One bitter cold day, while we were in school, Dad and Jase Perry butchered the hogs and our two pet lambs. I cried over my lamb, but Mom said it had to be done. There wasn't enough feed for them and the cow. And we needed the cow for milk.

George Brent, the farmer who lived around the bend on the gravel road, brought his tackle chain and pulley and helped with the butchering. Dad and Jase shared the meat and gave Mr. Brent pork tenderloin and lamb chops for his help and the use of his tackle.

Later on, Dad went to the Brents' and helped George cut and cord wood. George gave Dad money for it, but I think Dad would've rather had a cord of wood. He said that big heating stove ate wood faster than he could cut it by himself.

The attic room never got warm. Dad didn't believe in wasting heat or using up stove wood to heat a bedroom. When Mom called us to get up for school, we'd grab our clothes in our arms and race downstairs to crowd around the roaring red-hot stove to get dressed. The heat didn't spread far from the stove, so we had to stand close to get any benefit from the fire.

I was always the first one down the steps to find a spot next to the stove to put on my clothes.

One morning, I was standing too near the stove when I bent over to pull on my underwear. I yelled, leaped away like a scalded cat, and fell over Robert, who was sitting on the floor with his blanket around him. He began bawling and squalling, making more noise than I was.

Mom yelled, "My God, the baby!" and came running in from the kitchen to grab him up in her arms.

I was screaming, "Christ! I'm on fire! I've burned my butt off."

Mom slapped me across the mouth with the back of her hand. "You shut up and hush that talk, right now! Can't you see you're scaring the baby half to death? Get some clothes on and cover yourself. You're too big to be running around the house naked, showing everything you've got."

Julie grabbed a handful of lard out of the big can in the kitchen and rubbed it over the blisters. "Now it won't burn so bad and probably won't even scar." She giggled and patted on more lard. "Oh, Seely, it's a shame you ain't wider across the rear end. If you were, you'd have 'Hot Blast Air-Tight Florence' tattooed for life on your fanny."

The blistered bottom gave me a good excuse to lean forward at my desk that day and watch Clarence play with his little gray bugs, though. I tried not to look directly at him. It seemed to me that he had always sat in front of me. Any time I raised my eyes, I could see his thick red hair curling down over his dirty shirt collar. I don't think he ever washed his hair or took a bath. I know he never studied his lessons during study period, either.

He would sit at his desk and open his notebook; then he would lean way over and shake his hair to make the bugs fall out onto the paper. He kept a sharp lead pencil handy to jab and poke at them. If the teacher came down our aisle, Clarence would slam the book shut and mash all the bugs inside.

I don't know why, but that very evening, Clarence followed us home from school. No one asked him to, he just walked along behind us. When we opened the back door at home, he walked in and sat down.

Mom didn't know him. I suppose she thought we had finally found one friend in school and had brought him home with us. She added another potato and onion to the soup and set another plate on the table. Next to my place.

We each had our own place at the table, and we sat there for every meal. If one of us was absent, the chair was pushed up to the table. Tonight, Clarence had my chair and the kitchen step stool was in my place.

Mom had baked cornbread in a big round iron skillet, and a raspberry cobbler was cooling on the sideboard by the stove. Mom canned hundreds of quarts of berries in the summer, and we ate them one way or another all winter. Dad was partial to raspberry cobbler, and Mom usually made it as a special treat for him. I guess she figured if he had got a job that day it would be a celebration, and if he hadn't, it could be a consolation to him.

Clarence took a case knife from the table and measured the cuts of cobbler. Then he stuck his finger in the largest slice so no one else would eat it. He licked his finger and smacked his lips with pleasure afterwards.

Dad hadn't come home yet, but when supper was ready, Mom said, "You kids wash your hands and don't forget to use the soap. That's what we have it for."

Clarence splashed and sloshed the water in the wash basin and came to the table with his red curly hair slick as clay mud and his round freckled face shining in the lamp light.

Mom treated him like company and expected me to. She said, "Seely, talk to Clarence. You haven't said a word since you sat down at the table."

I said, "Hi, Clarence." As if I hadn't sat behind him

all day and walked home with him following along behind me.

He kept on chewing and didn't answer me.

"Stupid!" Julie said to me in a whisper.

Clarence stopped chewing, with his spoon halfway to his mouth and said, "Huh?"

I started giggling and Jamie caught the giggles from me; soon the whole table was in an uproar, with Clarence laughing as loud as the rest of us.

We wouldn't have dared to carry on that way if Dad had been home. He would have made quick work of clearing the lot of us from the table.

"You kids straighten up this minute," Mom finally said. "Do you want Clarence to think you act this way all the time?"

Clarence said, "No, ma'am," and slurped his soup.

I covered my face with my hands to hide my laughter, and my stool tipped over backward, knocking my bowl off the table as I fell.

Mom said, "Seely, go to the attic!"

I went.

Jamie came up after supper and said he would have brought me some cobbler, but there wasn't any left. Clarence had eaten two pieces, and Mom had offered him more. Then after Clarence had cleaned his plate, he handed it to Mom and said, "I dry the dishes at home. Dad says I can't wash them to suit him, and I don't have a mother to do it. If you like, I can dry your dishes for my supper."

Jamie said Clarence was stuttering and red as a beet, but his offer must have pleased Mom. She took to him right off the bat. She let him dry dishes for her and asked him to come back again when he left.

When I fell asleep, I was still trying to figure out ways to keep him from ever coming back to our house.

But the next night when I got home from school, there was Clarence in the kitchen dropping Mom's homemade noodles into a pot of boiling blackberries. I stood watching until the last noodle fell in the pot. Then Clarence excused himself and went outdoors.

I said, "Yuk . . . I'm not going to eat any dessert tonight. Not after that dirty old Clarence handled all the noodles."

Mom didn't turn from stirring the berries. "Many's the time I've had to send you away from the table with dirty hands."

"But he's different. All the kids laugh and make fun of him. Even the teacher says Clarence is a shame to the school."

"I don't ever want to hear tell of one of you kids making fun of someone because they're different. That day, I'll take a strap to you. Clarence never had a ma to care for him or see that he was raised properly. He's been shifted from pillar to post ever since he was a baby, living first with one relative and then another all his life, and not one of them wanting him. That would tend to make a body different."

"But does he have to come here ?. . ."

"Hush, he's coming in. Just keep quiet and eat your supper like everyone else."

I didn't tell Mom about the bugs Clarence grew in his hair. She would've taken lye soap and sulfur to all of us,

Clarence included, if she'd known. Mom couldn't bear to have any kind of bugs or a spider on the place.

I thought he had probably drowned them when he washed and slicked his hair down with water. But the next day at school, his hair had dried out and the bugs came alive and scurried across his notebook like tiny caged mice.

My hair had grown almost as long as Clarence's, so on Saturday Dad lined the boys and me up on a bench in the far end of the kitchen and started cutting our hair.

He cut mine last. He had barely begun cutting on one side when he commenced cussing. Dad usually cussed and roared when he had to cut my hair. He said it was like corn silk. It wouldn't lay down or stay in one place when he combed it or turn loose of the comb so he could clip it. But this time it was a different kind of swearing.

"Good diddlely damn, Zel. This kid is as lousy as a pet coon."

The other kids came running in to look.

"Damn it, you young'uns get in the other room. Can't have the whole bunch of you getting them. Wouldn't you know," he said to Mom, "if there was one louse in the county, this kid would find it and bring it home?"

Dad doused my head with coal oil, sulfur, and bacon grease, and Mom tied a hot towel around my head and pinned it so it wouldn't come loose. I figured that greasy mess was just feeding the little beasts, but I didn't care. Let them eat and grow fat!

I told Jamie, who was staring open-mouthed at me, "Now all my hair will probably fall out by the roots, and I'll be as slick bald-headed as old Bud Watson. I hope it does! Then I won't have to get my hair cut by that . . . that big baboon ever again."

Jamie turned and ran toward the other room. "Tattle-tale," I thought. "Go ahead and tell!" That wasn't any worse than some of the things Mom called Dad when she didn't like him. And today, I didn't like him.

Mom went up to Dicie Perry's to borrow a fine-tooth comb and was gone all afternoon. Dad said she could have made a comb in the time it took her to borrow one. When she got back, Julie held the lamp close, and Mom went over my head, hair by hair. When each strand was free and clear of bugs, Mom made us cross our hearts and raise our right hands and swear we wouldn't mention lice at school.

She said, "Dicie and me took care of the other buggy head in school, so we won't have to worry about you bringing more of them home."

She lifted a stove lid and threw the towels that had been around my head into the fire. "Everyone else's kids can carry lice, but I'll not have it said that one of mine ever did."

Monday morning, when I took my seat at school, Clarence was all ready seated at his desk. His hair was cut to a stubble, and his clean, pink scalp shone through where the scissors had taken big bites out of his hair. He turned and smiled at me as if we had something in common, and I noticed his plaid shirt had been washed and ironed for the first time.

chapter four

*J*ase Perry had said, when he moved us down to Greene County, that Dad could go to work cutting mine props and railroad ties for the mines like he did. But after Dad got there, he was told they were laying off men, not hiring them.

Dad cut wood for George Brent until he filled the woodshed, but other than that, Dad didn't go to work at all. It wasn't because he didn't look for it. He tried every rumor of work and went on from there. At the breakfast table he would say to Mom, "Zel, you'd better pack a clean shirt and a few things for me. It may be a spell before I get back."

Dad had been gone for nearly a week this time. Mom said she didn't expect him before Christmas, but every time she passed by the window, she pulled the lace curtain to one side and looked down the road toward town.

I guess Dad's being out of work was the reason the Women's Circle from the Flat Hollow Methodist Church brought the bushel basket of food stuff to our house on Christmas Eve. I don't know how they decide who needs a basket on Christmas, but however they figured it, Mom figured differently.

We had been trimming the Christmas tree when they came to our front door. Mom had said, right up to the last day, we couldn't have a tree. "There won't be a stitch of anything, no gifts of any kind to put under one this year," she said. "It's nonsense to have a bare tree and nothing to put under it."

But she changed her mind and gave in to us when she saw all the colored paper chains we had made and the angels we had cut from magazines and old greeting cards to hang on it. She even popped corn and threaded it on a long string, while Julie and Floyd Perry took a handsaw and went to the ridge to find a good cedar tree.

Cedar trees were about the only thing that would grow on the red clay knobs that rose out of the hills, jutting up between the oak and beech trees like a scab on the hillside. The cedars were scrubby, lopsided little trees with sharp spines and spurs that nipped and stung like a bee when we touched them. Everyone hated the cedars until Christmas; then they cut them and carried them home to set in a place of honor until the middle of January.

The Perrys had cut one for their Christmas tree, and Floyd said he knew right where to find another good one for us. But it took him and Julie a long time to find it. It was nearly dark before they came dragging it through the barnyard to the house.

Floyd nailed two flat boards crossways on the bottom of the tree and stood it in the corner of the front room. It wobbled back and forth and fell over. He stuck chips from the woodbox under the boards to level it, and laid big rocks on top of it all to keep the tree from tilting to one side.

Mom brought out an old white shirt of Dad's and spread it under the tree. She said it covered the rocks and boards and gave a natural look of snow for Christmas. We laughed when she buttoned the collar around the base of the tree and tucked the sleeves under the edges.

Mom lit two lamps and set one at each side of the tree, so we could see to trim it. We only decorated the front side where it showed. Mom was helping and seemed to be enjoying it as much as we were when someone knocked at the front door.

She handed Julie the string of popcorn and turned to open it. We should have barred the door or refused to answer, because Mom's Christmas spirit fled through the open door and away into the night.

Mom took the offered basket and held it in both hands, blocking the doorway. The women whispered a few words to her, and she thanked them as if they were all deaf. As soon as the door was slammed shut behind them, Mom flung the basket across the room and burst out crying.

"I'm not going to be treated like one of their shiftless,

no-good, hillbilly tribes. They don't need to think for one minute just because Rob ain't working regular, I can't manage. We'd have plenty right now if the root cellar hadn't frozen up solid and ruined the whole lot."

She wiped at her wet face with her apron tail and bent to gather up the scattered groceries. Jamie picked up six oranges that had rolled across the room and held them out to her. She looked at them as if she didn't know what they were. Then she said, "You kids eat them. And give one to Floyd."

Jamie passed the oranges around and put the one that was left over under the Christmas tree.

"Maybe Jase and Dicie would come down and eat dinner with us, tomorrow," she said more quietly. "Lord knows, there's enough here for both families. They might as well help us eat it."

She sent word home with Floyd that she was expecting them all to come to dinner next day.

As soon as Floyd left the house, Mom sent the boys upstairs to bed. She told Julie and me to rid up the front room before we went to bed, while she put the charity stuff out of her sight and got rid of the basket. "If I have to look at that tomorrow," she said, "I won't be able to eat a bite."

We gave the room a lick and a promise and then watched Mom as she moved between the basket on the table and the kitchen cabinet. She had loaded her arms with cans and boxes and turned toward the cabinet when Dad opened the kitchen door and stepped into the light.

He must have walked all the way from town. He

moved slowly like he could hardly put one foot in front of the other. He lifted the wooden box he was carrying on his shoulder, set it on the floor next to the woodbox, and heaved a great sigh of relief when he straightened.

He put his hands on the church charity basket. "What's all this?" he asked Mom.

"A poor box—" Her voice rose and broke.

I thought she was going to start crying again. She closed the cabinet door and started over, her voice flat and steady.

"The women from the church left it here earlier this evening. Floyd was here, so I told him to tell his folks to come for dinner tomorrow. Maybe I'll feel better about using it if I share it with Dicie."

"No reason for you to feel that way, Zel," Dad said. "It was given in good faith. We'll use it with that thought in mind, and share it if that's what you want."

"But Rob, it's for the poor!"

"I know." He moved nearer to her, but he didn't touch her. "I bought a crate of winesaps for the kids' Christmas. It was the only thing I could find for the money I had."

"Set them under the tree," Mom said. "We'll all enjoy them."

I didn't know we were poor. I knew we didn't have any money—Dad said so often enough—but we had food to eat and warm coats and shoes to wear. I thought the kids I went to school with were poor because they didn't have these things.

Julie and I each took one of the small, deep red apples

42

and went upstairs. They were hard and tangy and cracked like ice on a tree limb when we bit into them. The deep red of the skin faded and ran all the way to the core.

The next day, Dicie brought a fruit jar full of her homemade wine and two quarts of canned peaches to add to the meal Mom had fixed.

The little girls brought tin whistles that Jase had picked up some place to give them. The only time the whistles were out of their mouths was while they were eating.

To add to the racket, Floyd gave Jamie an old harmonica he had. Jamie breathed in and out, on the same keys—e-e-e-o-o-o, e-e-e-o-o-o— all day long.

Mom and Dicie talked quietly while they set the hot dishes on the table. Jase sat brooding with his feet propped on the apron of the heating stove and drank wine. Dad tried to talk to him, but Jase didn't seem to want to talk. He'd answer Dad, then go back to his brooding. Julie and Floyd held hands and walked close together in the yard. I seemed to be the only one who heard the shrill whistles and off-key whine of the harmonica as the kids raced through the house and jumped up and down the steps leading to the attic door.

Grownups must have an unspoken agreement that if your company's kids misbehave you'll yell at your own. I didn't think Mom or Dicie were paying any attention to the kids, but every time one of the Perry girls screamed, Mom hollered at me.

The Perrys went home as soon as they had finished

eating. The stillness they left behind seemed to press on my eardrums. Jamie sat on the attic steps, with his back resting against the door, and played his harmonica. But the sounds he made were soft and faint, almost like music. Dad sat quietly with Robert on his knees and smoked, while Mom and us girls cleaned up the kitchen. He seemed almost content. Not a bit the way he usually was since he'd been out of a steady job. I'd heard Mom tell Dicie that living with Dad lately was like sitting on a powder keg with a lit fuse; you never knew when he would blow up.

Mom was right about him blowing up. Dad would yell at us kids about things he didn't used to pay any attention to. No matter where we were or what we were doing, we were always in his way. He'd tell us to go to bed, then slam the attic door behind us. He'd blow up just at the sight of that attic door swinging open.

We'd hear Dad pacing from the kitchen to the front room for a while, then he'd slam the kitchen door behind him and walk hurriedly off toward the woods. Sometimes, he'd walk in the woods until after dark, or else he'd go to the Perrys' and talk to Jase and come home when we were asleep.

Jase had been laid off cutting timber nearly a month before Christmas, but he didn't go out looking for work, like Dad. He just lay around home or came over to our house. Jase was at our house a lot that winter. If he didn't come by for the long-green smoking tobacco, left hanging in the barn by the last people who had lived here, Dad would take the short cut and carry some to him. Dad's pipe tobacco came out of a cotton pouch with a drawstring top. He said long-green was too strong for him. It bit his tongue.

Dad and Jase went rabbit hunting if they had shells for the shotguns, or sat around drinking the homemade wine Dicie worked up during the summer, if they didn't. We could always tell which it had been. If Dad was asleep when we got home from school, they'd been in Dicie's wine; but if we had rabbit for supper, they had been hunting.

At the start of the second semester, Frieda and I recited lessons with the seventh grade, and Jamie was moved to the fourth, on condition. Teddy stayed where he was. He said he didn't mind. He liked the fourth grade. If the teacher had moved him to another class, he wouldn't have known anything.

Teddy knew his reader by heart and could do all the problems from the fourth-grade arithmetic book in his head. When we had ciphering matches on Friday afternoon, if Mr. Thompson stayed with adding and subtracting, Teddy could give the answers while the other kids were still writing the figures on the blackboard. Then he'd smile shyly at me from the front of the room.

Sometime during February, I had scarlet fever and we were quarantined at home. No one else caught it, but I had a red, blotchy rash and itched all over. After the rash and the redness went away, the skin peeled and flaked off my hands and feet like a snake shedding its winter skin in warm weather.

We worried about missing school for so long. Jamie fumed and fussed the most. Now that he was in the fourth grade, he was afraid he'd never get out. He said, "That grade is a jinx to the kids. If I don't pass this year, I'll still be there when I start to grow whiskers."

Eventually, the quarantine was lifted and we went back to school. Half the seats in the room were empty. It seemed a lot of the kids had caught the fever. Teddy's seat was among the empty ones, his books and papers were gone from his desk.

I waited until we were on our way to fill the water buckets. Then I asked Frieda where he was. She said Teddy had taken sick with the fever and died. He hadn't once complained of feeling bad. No one had even known he was sick.

"One morning Mama went to wake him for school and there he was, dead as a doorknob. I guess the Lord knew Teddy would never get past the fourth grade, so He took him out of school for good." Frieda's voice was flat and toneless as if death was not strange or unusual to her.

I had never known anyone who died. The nearest death had ever come to me had been when Dad butchered my pet lamb. I had cried then, and Dad said if I didn't hush my bawling he'd give me something to cry about.

I missed Teddy, but I didn't cry for him. It wasn't the same thing, at all.

Mr. Thompson moved another boy into Teddy's seat to fill out the row. Before long, it was as if Teddy had never been there. Nobody said his name. Only in my mind, he ran after me at recess and smiled shyly across the room during school hours.

chapter five

We'd gotten into the habit of stopping by the Perry house on the way to school to pick up the girls. One morning Dicie said we needn't bother for a spell. She didn't have anything fit to put in their dinner buckets, so she wasn't sending them to school.

I thought everyone had peanut butter and oleo they could put on biscuits or homemade bread, like Mom did for us. We nearly choked to death on it, but we had something in the lunch pail. Sometimes, when I couldn't swallow another bite, I'd feed a peanut-buttered biscuit to the old three-legged dog that hung around the schoolhouse begging food from the kids, just to see him try to get the peanut butter off the roof of his mouth. He seemed to know that all I had was peanut butter, and he

47

didn't come near me. He didn't like it any better than I did.

Before long Jase and Dicie sent Floyd and the girls to live at their grandmother's in Sullivan County. Dicie said the girls could go to school there, until Jase went back to work. Floyd said he was going to quit school and sign up for the CCC as soon as he was seventeen and send the money home to help his folks.

We had heard President Roosevelt make a speech over our battery radio about the CCC just a few nights ago. I guess Floyd had heard the same fireside chat. The President said he had formed the Civilian Conservation Corps to take the jobless boys off the streets and highways, put spending money in their pockets, and supplement their families' incomes. Meanwhile, these boys would be building the roads and bridges our country so desperately needed and protecting our national parks.

Dad had said he thought it was a good thing the President had done. The three C's taught the boys discipline and kept them out of trouble. "A lot of folks would be starving right now," he said, "if they didn't have a boy sending money home from camp every month for them to live on."

But still he tried to talk Floyd out of quitting school and joining the three C's. If a man was ever going to amount to anything, he had to have an education, Dad said. Money wasn't everything.

"When you ain't got it, it is," was Floyd's answer.

With Floyd and the girls away, Jase did more drinking than hunting. Jamie and I quit using the shortcut by their house. Every time we went by, Jase was staggering around in the yard trying to get his bearings or asleep and snoring on the cot on their screened-in porch. We never saw Dicie.

One night after Dad had been drinking wine all day with Jase, we heard a shotgun blast that echoed all through the hills before settling in the hollows. Dad jumped up and said, "That sounded like it came from Jase Perry's. I'd better get up there and see what has happened."

He grabbed his sheepskin coat from a hook by the back door and pulled his cap low over his eyes. "I'll be back as soon as I can," he told Mom. "No need to wait up for me."

Mom made us go to bed early, but I lay there for hours. The sound of low hushed voices woke me. It was dark outside, but Mom hadn't closed the attic door and a path of light came up the steps. Dad was saying, ". . . had wedged the double-barreled shotgun under his chin and used his bare big toe to pull the trigger. He blew his brains all over the bedroom wall where him and Dicie slept."

Mom murmured something I couldn't hear, and Dad said, "They took her away, too."

I heard him strike a match, and a few moments later I could smell the pipe smoke as it wafted up the stairs.

"She broke down, completely out of her head. When the sheriff and me got back to the house, Dicie was sitting flat on the floor beside Jase, humming and singing, them long black braids of hers swinging back and forth

49

as she kept time to the tune. Crooning to him, as if she was lulling a weary child to sleep."

"What's to become of those poor kids?" Mom asked.

"They'll be all right where they are. Their aunt and granny will see to their needs."

I heard him knock the doddle out of his pipe. "Better be sure our kids go by the road to school today. It'll be a spell before they finish up at the house."

The lights went out. I heard the long sigh of the bed springs and went back to sleep.

I felt like I had just closed my eyes when Mom called us to get ready for school. In the rush and confusion of getting dressed and in to breakfast, no one asked what had happened the night before.

I told Jamie on the way to school. "The reason Mom made sure we went around the road to school this morning is that Jase Perry blowed his head off last night with a shotgun."

He said, "I don't believe it. Seely, if you don't stop making up stories like that, no one is ever going to believe a word you say. People will say you're just a liar!"

"I am not lying! He did so, and there was blood and brains all over the place."

Jamie looked kind of greenish, like he was about to throw up. "I'm not going to walk with you today. You're . . . you're making me sick." He ran ahead and left me to walk the rest of the way alone.

I didn't really believe Jase had killed himself, either. I suspected if Jamie and I cut through the woods on our way home, we'd see Jase stumbling off toward the outhouse with his shoe strings untied and overall galluses hanging down around his hips, the same as usual.

Maybe I'd just dreamed I heard Dad and Mom talking last night, and Jase and Dicie would still be at their house if we stopped by.

But what if they weren't there? That was a chance I couldn't take, not with Jamie—and certainly not alone.

Eventually, the talk died down about Jase and Dicie. The men blamed it all on the Depression. They talked a lot about the Depression. They blamed the President and every man who had money when they didn't.

All I knew about the Depression was what I read in the dictionary. There were six definitions of depression, so I picked the second and last ones because they seemed to fit the way things were in Greene County, Indiana. "The state of being depressed," and "A period during which there is a decline in business."

In early April, Dad put out a truck garden patch, all in beans, back of the barn. He said, "If this Depression lasts much longer, we'll be eating beans three times a day."

School was out and the beans had started sprouting green leaves the size of a squirrel's ear above the red clay ground when Dad came home one evening and told Mom he'd heard tell that the government was starting up a factory at Crowe. Every man who showed up there ready for work had a job. "It may mean moving again," he said, "but I'm going to be the first man in the line to get a job."

"Seems a shame, don't it, Rob?" Mom said. "Jase Perry moved us down here where neither of you could work. If he'd only held out a while longer, he'd be moving us out to where there's a promise of work for everyone."

chapter six

Dad left before daylight the next morning, walking to Crowe, and was gone for nearly a week. Mom sang as she cleaned the house from top to bottom and wondered aloud what kind of place Dad would find for us in Crowe. She was sure he'd get a job. "If there's work to be had," she said, "your daddy will find it."

Dad found a job. He told us all about it as soon as he got home. He said he had walked most of the way down there, but he'd hitched a ride back home with another man who had gone to Crowe for a job. "He'll pick me up here early Monday morning," Dad said, "but I don't know when I'll be able to get home again."

"What about a house for us, Rob?" Mom asked. "Couldn't you find a place for us to live there?"

Dad said the government had thrown together some shacks for the workers to live in, but they weren't fit for a man's wife and children. "The only people who will live in them are hillbillies from Kentucky," Dad said, "and painted streetwalkers."

I waited for Mom to ask which state streetwalkers came from, but she didn't. She never said much of anything, but her lips turned down at the corners and her eyes lost the happy, expectant shine they had worn for the past few days.

I knew she had been counting the days until we could bid good-bye to the hills and hollows and live, as she put it, like civilized human beings again. Mom told Dad it was hard for her to stay behind with us kids while he shook the red clay from his feet and went out of the hills to live.

"Zel, it's a job. A man has to go where the work is. And I'll feel better about it if I know you and the young'uns are here in your own house."

"All right, Rob," Mom said. "I'll stay. But I'll tell you right now, I don't like it."

No more was said about moving. Mom got Dad's things together so he'd be ready to leave when his ride to Crowe came by on Monday morning. When we tried to help her, she snapped, "Get out from under my feet and leave me be. You kids are more hinder than help."

We spoke softly and moved quietly out of her way.

We didn't see Dad before he left, and we didn't see him again for a long time. But we kids didn't miss him very much. There was a lot to see and do in the woods around us.

Spring seemed to come to Greene County at the same time Dad got the job in Crowe. It seemed like just overnight the trees leafed out in their many shades of green, and in the woods dogwood and rosebud bloomed. Their deep pink and white blossoms blazed a colorful trail haphazardly up and down the hills. I could understand how the county had got its name; even the grass looked greener here than anywhere else.

The singing and chirping of birds awoke us at first light, and we'd go out and wade through heavy morning dew, exploring the country around us. Wild yellow canaries, with dabs of black painted on their wings, darted and swooped overhead. We ran into the thickets and buckbrush after them, trying to find where they nested and hatched their young. We told Mom if we could find their nest, we'd bring her a canary.

She said, "You leave them wild things be. If you put your hands in a nest, the mother won't come back, and the little ones will starve to death."

Paths and trails, which had lain hidden on the bare red ground, appeared when the grass started growing beside them. We followed the paths to wild strawberry patches and thickets of wild plum, white with blossoms. Up near the empty Perry house, we found spearmint, thick and fragrant, growing wild around an ever-flowing pool of clear, cold spring water gushing out of the hillside. We chewed sprigs of spearmint leaves and cupped the spring water in our hands for a drink. The water was always colder and sweeter after chewing the mint leaves.

We found the first wild flowers in the woods and carried crowfoots, lamb's-tongues and white kitten britches, limp and wilted, home to Mom. We gathered moss, soft and thick as lamb's wool, and held it close to our faces, just to touch something beautiful. Then we placed it back on the ground and packed the grainy black woods' earth gently around it so it wouldn't die and we could come back to it another day.

Jamie and I wandered along the creek bank where touch-me-nots made a patchwork quilt of yellow, orange, and green down to the water's edge. We skirted the mass of flowers and fished broken limbs and twigs from the creek, then waited for the muddied water to clear so we could see the slate and sandstone that lay on the riverbed.

When we came to the footlog, we saw that dead leaves and broken branches had drifted and collected there, forming a dam under the footlog. Small streams of water were flowing slowly at each side, but the main stream was being held back, making a pool above the footlog. Soon it would overflow and cover our makeshift bridge.

The next day, Jamie and I went to Lick Crick to clear away the rubbish that had lodged under the log and free the trapped river. Before long, the water was rushing downstream again and out of the hills to join White River in the bottom lands.

All the rivers that ran through the hills of Greene County were clean, clear, and fast running, as if in a hurry to get out of the hills and see the world; a world not hemmed in on all sides by tall trees and small mountains.

We would get home after dark, our clothes wet and muddy from playing along the creek bank and covered with sticktights and cockleburrs. We'd stop at the barn, light the lantern, and hurriedly strip the burrs from our clothes before going on to the house for supper.

Once we asked Mom to bring Robert and walk in the woods with us, but she said she was as close to the woods as she ever wanted to be. "I don't see what you two kids can find to do in them hills and hollows," she said.

One morning, Julie came with us. I gathered bunches of redbud and dogwood blossoms, and Julie broke long branches of waxy paw-paw leaves and scarlet-veined sumac to add greenery. Then we hurried home to give the fruit jar full of flowers to Mom.

She accepted, silent and tight-lipped. Not even spring-time could lessen Mom's dissatisfaction with the place or make her any happier to be there without Dad. She didn't see the beauty of green things growing from the red dirt. All she ever saw was the mud we tracked into the house from the clay paths that led up to the door.

She said she didn't know how Dad could go away and leave her in these hills with nothing but trees around her and mud underfoot. He could have found a place out of this dark hollow, if he'd tried.

She blamed the hills for Jase's death and Dicie's break-down. "If they had been any place except in these god-forsaken hills, they could've faced these hard times and seen them through," she said. "They'd known trouble before and stood up to it." Now that Dicie was gone, she was all alone down here. She guessed she didn't have a friend in the world. She clung to her aloneness and re-fused to make friends. The ones who came to call and pass the time of day with her seldom came back after the first time.

George and Clara Brent came by faithfully, once or twice a week, when they were driving to McVille or to the city. Mom spoke civil enough to them, but she was brusque with her answers and cut their visits short with excuses of work to be done. After they'd gone, Mom would mutter, "I've got better things to do than listen to Clara Brent's gossip and tall tales."

We gave up trying to make Mom feel better.

The leaves Julie had picked for Mom from the sumac bush had given her a bright red rash from wrists to elbows. In no time at all, her arms were swollen to nearly twice their normal size and covered with a mass of tiny water blisters. Mom smeared a baking soda paste over Julie's arms and wrapped strips torn from an old sheet around each one.

Before the end of the week, Julie had the poison on both legs, too, all the way up to her straddle. Mom said Julie was too big and too old to be traipsing around the country. She'd had no business out in the woods in the first place!

Mom fussed and complained as she gently washed the open sores, applied salve, and changed the bandages.

I said Julie looked like one of the Egyptian mummies I'd seen in my history book, only they were bandaged neater. They didn't have lumps and knots with long strings hanging out on their arms and legs.

Mom snapped at me. "Missy, if you don't like the way I do this, maybe you'd better get one of them Egyptians to show me how they do it! Lord knows, I could use some help."

I guess He did. Early on Monday morning, He sent the Brents by our house on their way to the county seat. They asked, the way they always did, if we needed anything brought out from town. We never did, because anything Mom needed she could get on credit at Bud Watson's general store in McVille.

Clara took one look at Julie and said, "Zel, you'd better get ready and take this girl in to see a doctor. My trading can wait. There ain't room in that car for all four of us, so I'll stay here with your young'uns until you and George get back."

Julie looked ready to cry. Robert was bawling and hanging on to Mom's skirt. Jamie came and stood close by me, and I put my arm around him. His brown eyes were wide with fright. To take someone to a doctor's office was enough to scare anybody. The only time one of the hill families ever saw a doctor was when he came, after all the homemade remedies had failed, to write or sign a death certificate. We were sure we would never see Julie again. The doctor would sign the papers, and they would bury her.

Clara took Robert on her lap in the rocking chair and talked and rocked until he quieted down. He cuddled into her soft rolls of flesh and listened to her stories. Robert would be five years old in the fall, but he was small for his age and acted a lot younger.

Clara didn't know what to do with us kids. She held Robert on her lap and wouldn't let Jamie and me out of her sight. When she went to the kitchen to make peanut butter and bread for us, we had to be there with her.

She opened the cupboard doors and clucked over the dishes Great-grandmother Curry had left to Mom and handled them as carefully as fresh-laid eggs. Mom wouldn't have liked her going through things in the house while she was away. I didn't know what she'd say when she noticed that Clara had cleaned the pie safe in the kitchen and polished the dull turquoise door panels until they shone like a pewter pot in a mudhole.

Clara had lit the coal-oil lamps and started supper before we heard George's car throwing gravel as it turned into the barnyard, bringing Mom and Julie home.

We weren't allowed to touch Julie or use anything she touched. I had to sleep in Jamie's bed with him and Robert so I wouldn't catch her poisoning. I told Mom I wouldn't show my straddle to a doctor or anyone else, even if I did get poisoned.

She said, "I don't think we have to worry about you, Seely; poison kills poison."

I guess she was right. Nothing ever poisoned me.

We had an old two-holer outhouse down the path past the root cellar, but while Julie had the poison, she had to use the china chamber pot, the rose-flowered one that matched the bowl and pitcher on Mom's dresser. Every evening Julie carried the pot at arm's length to empty it Then she washed it and brought it back upstairs. Mom cautioned her daily to be careful of how she handled it, but Julie still swung it by two fingers like a tin slop bucket.

One morning Julie rushed over and sat with all her weight on the pot. The pot split and left her sitting in the middle of a puddle and broken china.

I laughed, but I thought Mom would probably bust a blood vessel or else beat Julie to death when she saw the mess on the floor.

She didn't. She cleaned the floor and didn't say a word or lay a hand on Julie.

But Julie couldn't keep quiet. "That old pot was cracked long before I ever sat on it."

Mom pressed her lips tighter than ever and gave an extra hard swipe with the mop. "That old pot, as you call it, was your Great-grandmother Curry's chamber pot. I carried the set with me when I married your father. I might have known you kids couldn't keep your hands off it, and it would get broken."

Great-grandmother Curry had been dead for a hundred years, I'll bet, but Mom still took care of her things and spoke of her as if she expected Great-grandmother Curry to walk through the door at any time and find a chip in one of her dishes or a speck of dust on the walnut stand table.

Julie said, "My hands didn't touch it. All I did—"

Mom whirled around, the mop still clutched threateningly in her hands. I ducked my head and ran from the room.

chapter seven

*M*om resigned herself to staying in Greene County, but she was a changed person. I could hear her walking the floor and moving about at night, long after us kids were in bed. Each morning she would look even more tired and worn than she had the day before. Her body seemed to shrink and bend in the middle like an old woman's.

She said she was trapped in these everlasting hills and there was no way out for her. Day and night she could feel the hills closing in on her, squeezing the very life from her body. Once her eyes filled with tears, and she said, "I have nothing to look forward to, nothing at all."

Dad stayed at Crowe. He came home whenever he could bum a ride with one of the men who was driving up our way. The first time he came home, Jamie ran to him as soon as he walked through the door and began to tell him all the things we'd been doing since he'd been away. Dad shushed him and asked Mom, "Doesn't this kid ever hush up?" He pushed Jamie away impatiently and began to talk to Mom.

He never stayed long. He would give Mom some money and his dirty clothes to wash and be gone before noon the next day. He never seemed to notice us kids unless we walked between him and the lamplight while he was reading the newspaper. We were just as happy that he didn't. We knew we were more apt to get the back of his hand than a pat on the head if we were within touching distance. Only Robert dared to approach him. He would climb on Dad's lap and sit quietly content, while Dad read or smoked his pipe and talked about his work.

Mom's eyes and face were soft and tender when Dad kissed her good-bye, but by the time she had finished scrubbing his heavy pants and shirts on the board and put them out to dry on the line, her lips would be drawn to a thin slit and her dark eyes hard and snapping beneath a frowning brow.

In the early part of May, Mom said with more spirit and determination than we had heard in a long time, "Maybe we'll eat beans all winter, but we're going to have fresh green vegetables this summer."

I looked at the field of burdock, dandelions, and ragweed that was our yard and wondered how on earth she could ever get a garden planted there.

She sent Jamie and me to clear the fence row where some rhubarb had gone to seed, its bushy yellow blossoms standing higher than the crooked old pickets, and the smartweed and wild geranium crawled across the ground and lay heavily underfoot.

Then, while she was still fired with the vision of green vegetables growing plentifully at hand, she asked George Brent to bring his horse and plow a garden spot for her. There was no offer of pay and none was asked. When the weeds were turned under, he worked the plowed ground with a harrow. But there were still big lumps and clods left where the harrow had missed them.

Mom and Julie took turns with the spade and hoe, breaking the hard clods of dirt, and I raked the ground into a pliable patch ready for planting as soon as George brought the seeds out from the city.

Mom traded a handmade quilt she had spent years piecing and sewing together to Clara for enough money to pay for the seed potatoes, corn, and tomato plants George brought to her.

Ever since the day Clara had stayed with us kids while Mom took Julie to a doctor in town, Clara had tried to wheedle Mom out of our junky old furniture or sometimes a dish that had taken her fancy. I couldn't imagine why she'd want them. She had the money to go and buy anything she fancied, brand new.

While George was laying out the garden rows, Clara sat in the front room and rocked and talked. She ran her hands over the cool marble top of the old black walnut stand table and said, "Now, Zel, if you ever want to get rid of this, let me know. Not that I'd have any earthly use for it, but I'd like to have this lovely old piece."

Mom smiled, pleased that Clara admired the table or else because she knew she had something Clara didn't have and couldn't get. She had carried in two cups of coffee from the pot on the back of the stove and set one near Clara's hand.

"Oh, I don't think I'll ever have need to part with that stand table. I expect to give it to one of my girls when they marry."

I looked at the old table and thought to myself, "I don't have to worry. It won't last that long!"

Jamie came running across the porch, dodging the loose boards, and in the front door. He was so excited and out of breath he couldn't speak.

Mom said, "Settle down, Jamie, and take a deep breath before you have a spell. Whatever it is can wait that long."

"George found a whole nest of copperheads," he said. "He's killing them with the hoe. You should see, they're all over the garden. Big ones and little ones crawling everywhere!"

He turned and ran back to the garden.

Mom said, "I'd better see about him. He's apt to be sick from all the commotion going on."

Clara pulled her weight from the rocker, and we followed Mom to the plowed ground. Jamie stood watching, pale and tense, as George gave a final whack with the hoe to one rusty spotted snake still moving near his feet. One by one, he lifted the dead snakes on the hoe blade and threw them over the fence onto the gravel road. The last and largest one of all, he picked up by the tip of its tail and snapped its head off before he tossed it onto the road with the others.

He rubbed his hands on his coveralls, then pulled a big handkerchief from his pocket and wiped the sweat off his face. "I probably plowed them buggers up yesterday. But they were sluggish and didn't start moving around until the sun came up this morning and warmed their bed. You kids will have to watch where you're tramping. When you run onto one nest of copperheads, there's bound to be another nearby."

There seemed to be no end to the hidden dangers just lying in wait for us kids behind every tree and beneath each blade of grass. Mom warned us about the five-leaf poison ivy vine, the bottomless sinkholes that could swallow us and never leave a trace of our whereabouts, and snakes. We were to be especially cautious about watching for snakes.

She said, "If you kids see a snake, listen for a rattle. A rattler will warn you, but a copperhead is blind and sneaky. They'll strike without warning."

Last summer, Julie's cat had been bitten by a snake, and it swelled up and died. Dad said he didn't know where the damn cat could've gone to get snake bit. All the snakes on the farm were harmless, caught more mice around the barn than the damn cat.

Now, from the way Mom spoke, there were only two kinds of snakes in Greene County, both deadly poison; and if one didn't make any noise, it was a copperhead.

After George stepped off the garden rows, staked them, and strung binder twine so we could plant in a straight line, he and Clara went home. He left most of his garden tools, in case we needed them to finish working the garden.

I know Mom must have had other gardens; she knew all about raising vegetables. But I couldn't ever remember another one. She had to tell us kids everything that had to be done and how to do it.

She showed Julie and me how to set out tomato and cabbage plants. I dug the holes, Julie poured water for the roots to drink; and on her hands and knees, Mom set the plants and tamped the soft earth around them. Every so often, she would stand and place both hands flat to the small of her back and stretch as far as she could reach. She would smile at us and say, "Well, this ain't plantin' peas, is it?"

Then she would kneel and set the next plant.

We sowed lettuce, radishes, green onions, and two rows of sweet corn close to the house. Mom said, "The sweet corn is going to be right handy up here. I can get a mess of roastin' ears just by reaching through the kitchen window." Then she laughed.

I guess that's what made the garden so special to us. Mom didn't laugh much or smile on us often these times. But that day, she did both.

At dusk, Mom called Jamie and Robert from where they were playing in wet clay, and the five of us walked to the house together. Mom was the happiest I'd seen her since the day we moved down here.

Late the next day, Mom marked rows at one end of the plowed ground for the potato patch. Then she showed Jamie and me how to cut the eyes and peelings for seed and save the rest for soup. "It's a blessing that school is out." Mom said. "I'd never get this garden planted without your help."

Mom gave us two dull paring knives and left us with a gunny sack full of potatoes. "When you get the kettle full for cooking, quit cutting, and start planting. Do it like I showed you—a couple of feet apart and cover them well."

When they were all cut and sorted, Mom took the pan of potatoes to the house to start supper, and we started planting the sprouts and peelings. I dug shallow holes about a foot apart, and Jamie dropped in the seeds. Then we covered them with a thin layer of dirt and stamped it down with our bare feet.

We worked at a snail's pace, trying to time it so we would finish planting about the same time the potato soup was done. We figured if we took small mouthfuls and swallowed slowly, it would be too dark to work in the garden after supper.

Every morning by first light, we were out in the garden in our nightclothes, checking the rows to see if anything had come up, long before it was time for us or the plants to be up. It seemed like the weeds popped up overnight. At the first sight of green growing in the garden, we ran to tell Mom the corn was coming up. She took one look and said it wasn't corn, it was ragweed. We wanted to pull all the weeds, but she said she'd pull the weeds until we could tell the difference between them and a stalk of corn. She shook her head as if she couldn't believe our ignorance and went to the kitchen to fix our breakfast.

One morning Mom called us, and Julie and Jamie went in to the house at once. Breakfast was ready. I could smell the ham and biscuits, and I knew Mom would have thick, creamy ham gravy to put over the biscuits; but I had to go to the outhouse first. Instead of going back to the house and taking the path from the kitchen door, past the root cellar, to the outhouse, I lifted my nightgown above my knees and cut catty-cornered through the tall, dewy weeds.

I was watching for prickly thistles, trying to miss the nettles, and didn't see the snakes until I stepped on them. A big brown snake was coiled like a piece of rope protectively over a nest of soft-skinned white eggs. Baby snakes, the size of overgrown fishing worms, were slowly working their way through small cracks in the shells.

I didn't breathe and I didn't hear a sound from the snakes. "My God, I thought, copperheads!" and started screaming.

I forgot I had to go to the toilet. I whirled around and started running through the weeds and thistles straight for the kitchen door. I was midway through the high weeds when I saw Jamie. He had run out of the kitchen door, and his bare arms were covered with scalding hot ham gravy. Almost at once, he dropped down and began to wipe it off frantically on the grass.

I didn't know what had happened, but I caught his hands and lifted him to his feet. Mom rushed to help him.

The burns from the gravy were deep and raw where Jamie's arms bent at the elbow. Mom wrapped clothes soaked in soda and cold well water around them. She said all her children would probably be crippled one way or another, living down in this hellhole, where a body couldn't get a doctor until he died nor a preacher to read over him when he did.

After she finished dressing Jamie's burns, she said, "Now, Missy, what were you screaming and yelling about? You scared Jamie something fierce, so he knocked over that hot gravy. He could've been scalded to death. It's just a miracle he's not burned a lot worse than he is. Well?..."

She was waiting for me to answer. I had forgotten the snakes. "I stepped on a bunch of snakes hatching in the high weeds." It was little more than a whisper.

"If this is one of your stories, I'll take a strap to you, Seely." Mom opened the screen door. "Come and show me where you saw them."

We walked by the garden where Mom took a hoe from the fence to clear the thistles from our way and kill the snakes, if she found any.

They were still lying just as I'd seen them. The parent snake sluggish and sleepy with the small ones squirming over and under it as they left the soft white egg sacks.

Mom took one look, snorted, and turned back the way we had come. "All that fuss and pother over a little garter snake and a nestful of babies." She tossed the hoe toward the garden fence where it caught and swung a few times before it fell to the ground, blade side up. It was no time to remind her that we'd been told never to leave a hoe with the blade bare.

I put the hoe back on the fence and ran after her in time to catch the tail end of her words. "You've got to control yourself, Seely, or you'll send me to an early grave with your tomfoolery."

It seemed like I was forever promising to behave myself, not to yell at Robert, not to scream at field mice, lower my voice, and stop telling big stories! Mom said the truth was good enough, I didn't need to embroider everything I said.

"I thought they were copperheads. I really did. They didn't make a sound, and there could have been a whole colony of them just waiting for me."

"You thought? Seely, you don't think. You speak without thinking and yell before you're hurt. This time it was Jamie who got hurt. Maybe if you have to take care of him, it will teach you to think the next time. From now on, you're to be responsible for Jamie."

She talked and I listened to her. For once, I paid strict attention to every word. A bad scare like this might bring on one of Jamie's fits, she said, and I was old enough to help him and should know what to do if he had one when we were alone. "There's nothing to be afraid of. Just be sure he can't bite his tongue or choke on it. The fits don't last more than a minute, and most of the time he knows they're coming on and can tell you."

Jamie didn't have fits often, and I hoped my yelling wouldn't make that kind of trouble for him now.

It didn't.

Though Mom was afraid Jamie's arms would be stiff or crooked because she couldn't take him to a doctor, they healed fast and straight. In time, only a few pink scars remained to remind me of my foolishness.

chapter eight

*B*eginning that morning, Jamie was my responsibility. I stayed with him and took care of him. I did my share of the chores and his, too, as long as his arms were bandaged. While I cut and raked weeds along the fence row and fed the chickens, Jamie sat in the shade of the big maple tree, rubbing Clover Leaf salve on his arms. And while I carried buckets of water down the garden row, watering the plants as I went, Jamie's shadow lay alongside mine as he followed silently, waiting for me to be done with the work.

I would hurry through our chores so we could roam the hills and hollows together. There was always a new stand of woods Jamie wanted to explore, or a red clay bank to dig into for Indian arrowheads. Jamie had a cigar box almost full of arrowheads now, but still he searched for more. On a ledge, away under the big rock on the other side of the creek, he kept his cigar box of treasures. My notebook was stuck between two rocks a little to one side of Jamie's ledge. I had taken it with me once to write in while we watched the day change colors, and I left it there when we went back to the house.

As the days grew longer, Jamie and I spent more and more time in the woods or in the room under the big rock. The woods were our playground, and the cave was our resting place till it was time to go home.

On some of the trees near our cave, dried black grape-vines the size of a man's arm hung free from the top branches or twisted over the larger limbs and down the trunk of the tree. We found by holding a vine in both hands, like a baseball bat, and taking a running jump into the air, the grapevine would lift us high off the ground. Then we'd wrap our legs around the vine and fly through the air like great wingless birds, far out and over the gully behind Lick Crick.

We had discovered that people around these parts threw their junk and trash into the gully. Sometimes good junk. Jamie and I rummaged through the junk hole and found bright amber bottles, pretty colored dishes that were cracked only a little, and old books that we carried up to the cave. We set the amber bottles on the flat rocks up and down each side of the opening, and late in the day they caught the light of the sun and reflected on every side of the cave.

One hot day followed the other with no sign of a break in the heat. After the sun went down behind the hills, we'd draw water from the well and water the garden. Sometimes, we would lug the buckets from Lick Crick and fill the rain barrel and wash tubs. With every bucket of water drawn from the well, Mom would say, "If this hot spell doesn't break soon, I'm afraid this old well will go dry or get too low for us to use. I don't know what we'd do without drinking water."

The cow had gone dry during the first hot spell of spring, and we didn't have any milk to drink. Mom bought canned milk and complained that "feeding a dry cow was as bad as paying for a dead horse. Neither one was of any earthly good to anybody."

Once in a while, thunder clouds, black and rumbling, would roll in from the west, and we'd have a gully-washer of a storm. Water roared down from the hills and rain stood ankle deep in the garden rows. But by nightfall, the dry, cracked red clay had absorbed all the moisture.

After these cloudbursts, steam rose from the ground and the muggy heat sapped our strength. We sat in the shade or catnapped while Mom rocked and fanned herself on the front porch.

Most of the gardening was done late in the day after the sun had lost its power to scorch us or burn the fresh-turned earth. Fighting bugs off the plants and keeping the weeds from taking over the garden was a job for everybody. One day we killed bugs, and for the next two days we cut weeds.

It was our day to weed the beans. Jamie and I worked until we couldn't see the end of the bean row for the sweat in our eyes. Then Jamie laid the hoe, blade down, in the dirt along the unfinished row, and we ran down the path to Lick Crick.

The wide swimming hole under the willow trees was the promised coolness we had waited for all day. We stripped off our clothes and dived into the creek, head first and bare naked.

Jamie splashed me and shoved my head under the surface. I came up spluttering, spitting muddy water, and trying to duck him.

"That's not fair! I wasn't ready yet!"

He laughed and swam out of my reach, turned and splashed water in my face. He caught hold of a willow limb that hung low over the water and pulled himself into the tree. Then he made a belly whopper into the creek beside me.

I went under again.

I gagged and gasped for breath and wiped the creek water from my eyes. When I could see, I waded to the shallows and climbed the slick, red bank to fall breathlessly into the tall horseweeds that grew thick along Lick Crick.

Jamie splashed and whooped his way out and lay laughing on the ground beside me. He picked up his shirt and dried my hair before we dressed. If Mom saw my wet hair, she'd know I'd gone in swimming naked. She'd harp on it for a week and might forbid me to go swimming in the creek, dressed or not, if she knew.

Dressed again, we ran through the dusk trying to catch the flickering, green-tailed lightning bugs that flitted just

76

overhead, and choked on our laughter when we tripped and fell.

Mom said we were growing wild as a couple of woods' colts, but she didn't say stay home. She just said, "Stay with your brother, Seely." And she never noticed when we left.

Once when we were hunting a different place to swing on a grapevine—a longer, stronger one with a deeper hollow to span—we crossed the ridge and saw a big white house sitting all by itself between two hills. There was no smoke coming from the chimney and not a soul around the place. Just another big empty house.

I wanted to get closer, to look inside, but Jamie wouldn't hear of it. He said he'd heard in school there were a lot of empty houses back in the hills. People just packed up and moved away overnight, leaving behind what they couldn't carry out on their backs.

I wondered where all the others lived who came to school. Somehow, I'd never talked to them much. We hadn't seen them since school let out in April. I wished someone would move into one of the empty houses in the hills near us. I felt as if Jamie and I were the only kids around. I missed Frieda and her talking to and from the well. I'd had to listen closely to understand everything she said, but she knew an awful lot I couldn't find in books. Even if Frieda had come to see me and asked me to go to her house, Mom wouldn't have let me go there.

Julie's friend, Nancy Ann Arthur, came to see her once or twice a week, but we seldom saw anyone else.

We didn't see many cars on the road in front of our

house, either. When the Brents' car passed by our place, Jamie and I ran to the picket fence to watch it out of sight, just as we'd seen other kids do the day we had moved in.

The mailman drove by every day, and sometimes an old beat-up truck, with its springs sagging under a load of battered household stuff being moved in or out of the hills, would stop and get water for the steaming radiator.

We would run and hide behind the house, in case they were gypsies, until we heard the truck chugging on down the road.

Mom was sure every stranger who stopped was a gypsy, spying out families where they could steal the kids. Dad said gypsies weren't stupid. They wouldn't want her kids! "A lot you know about it," Mom snapped, and continued to watch us like a chicken hawk at a brooder house door whenever a stranger came by.

I think I would've talked to these strangers if Mom hadn't kept us away from them. I wanted someone who would talk to me. Mom talked, but she said, "Seely, do this," or, "Seely, don't do that." And she never told me why. I needed someone who could give me a reason for things.

Jamie didn't talk much at all. He was just there in case I had something to say. We could be together all day and not speak three words. But I could touch Jamie; like Teddy, we could communicate.

Sometimes, Jamie reminded me of Teddy with his quiet ways and gentle manner. I knew Teddy had liked the hills, and I often wished he could have stayed here a little longer to roam the hills and hollows with Jamie and me. Once, I remarked to Jamie that I bet Teddy could've got out of the fourth grade all by himself, if God had kept his nose out of it.

Jamie had said, "Seely, you'll go to hell for finding fault with God. And if Mom ever hears you, you'll get worse than that for it."

chapter nine

We left the front gate at daylight on Sunday and walked fast all the way to get to church before the last bell rang for service. Mom had sworn she'd never set foot inside the church after the Flat Hollow Methodist Church women left the Christmas basket at our house, but not a Sunday passed that we weren't there. As we hurried along the dusty, graveled road, other women and children joined us. By the time we reached the church house, there would be more than a dozen kids running, fighting, falling, and crying, while their moms and mine calmly exchanged bits of news and the latest gossip.

Clara Brent would smile and wave as she and George passed us in a cloud of dust. He'd slow down and nod at the women as if apologizing for riding while they walked or else for the choking dust his automobile stirred up on the road.

The women smiled and waved back, then said nice things about the Brents. No one seemed to blame them for being well off or driving a car while the others had to walk to church.

I guess most of the people knew they would be riding with the Brents if George had room in the car to carry them. They were glad George and Clara had money and a car, because any time they needed anything they knew they could always borrow from the Brents.

No one could have been more surprised than Mom when Clara came to our house early one morning to borrow from her.

I had just started down the first row of potato vines, knocking the bugs off with a stick and burying them in the soft dirt with my big toe, when George and Clara drove into the barnyard. George helped Clara out of the car, then he went to the barn, and Clara came to the potato patch.

"Seely, how would you like to come over to my house and help out for a spell? This heat has got me plumb tuckered, and I'm behind with everything."

I smiled and dug my toes in the soft dirt. "If I had my druthers, I guess I'd druther do anything than bug potatoes."

She laughed and said, "I'll speak to your mom about it," and went on to the house.

I guess the idea of Clara Brent borrowing something from her stunned Mom long enough for her to say I could go. Jamie could bug potatoes by himself for a while. And she supposed she could spare me for an hour or so.

Jamie hung on the gate, looking as if he had lost his last friend, and I climbed into the car with George and Clara and bounced off down the road to their house.

That first day, Clara showed me how to make a bed: to fold the corners of the sheet under the mattress; lay the pillows end to end so the lacy border would hang over the side; then spread the silky coverlet neatly over the whole thing. I changed the same bed three times before I finally did it to suit her.

Clara showed me how to set her table, and while she taught me, she talked. My wish had come true. Clara had a vast store of information, and she gave it all to me. She told me about everyone and everything in our neck of the county. I didn't even have to ask.

My head was spinning as I tried to digest everything she had told me. After the dishes were washed and put away, Clara gave me a quarter and said, "Run along home, now. But come back in a couple of days. I want you to help me do some cooking."

I went out the back door, past the barn and woodpile, and cut through their cornfield. Their corn was a lot higher than ours, but it was full of weeds. Mom said our corn should be knee high by the Fourth of July. It only had about a week to make it.

Most of the time, I was just glad to be with Clara. As long as I was helping her, I didn't have to work in the garden. Luckily, there wasn't much to do in the garden now or Mom might not have let me go. We were using the lettuce, radishes, and green onions. I even carried some to Clara when I went to her house to help with whatever she was doing that day.

We had fresh green peas, too, and we liked them creamed. Dad hadn't been home once for creamed peas or fresh garden salad, but today was the Fourth of July, and he was home from Crowe for the weekend. Mom said it was a good thing Dad had come home today. The vines had dried up so fast, this would be the last mess of peas she'd be able to get this summer.

Whenever Dad came home, Mom fixed something special for him and used her good dishes on the table. When he was away, we had soup and cornbread or biscuits and beef gravy from chipped plates and bowls that came in the big sacks of Robin Hood flour.

Today, Mom dug a few potatoes, no bigger than marbles, and creamed peas and potatoes together for supper. She said they would go further that way. There was fried chicken and wilted lettuce on the table; green onions and red and white radishes lay side by side in great-grandmother Curry's old cut-crystal relish dish. The wild strawberries that Julie and I had picked during the morning were soaking in simple syrup, ready for the tiny shortcake biscuits warming in the oven.

Dad had no more than got seated at the table when he said to Mom, "You couldn't keep your hands off the potatoes and wait for them to get big enough to eat before you dug into them, could you? It's the same thing every year."

83

I don't know why he was scolding her. He knew as well as we did that Mom had dug into the potatoes today especially for him.

She pretended not to hear him. "Let's say grace, children, and thank God our garden has given us food for today."

We bowed our heads. Since Mom had been going to prayer meeting every Wednesday night with Clara and dragging us to church on Sunday, we had to give thanks for every bite we swallowed, whether we felt thankful or not.

When thanks had been given and every plate around the table was filled to the brim, Dad said to Mom, partly in jest but mostly in earnest, "You'd do better to thank the good Lord your back held up to hoe the weeds. Seems to me you could've found a more likely piece of ground if you wanted to grow vegetables. But no, you had to pick the weediest damn spot I've ever laid eyes on to put out your garden."

He said it lightly, but Julie didn't take it lightly. She pushed her chair back from the table. Tears of anger spilled over on her face as she ran toward the stairs.

Dad called, "Where do you think you're going? Come back here and finish your supper."

Julie didn't hold back or hesitate for a moment. He left the table and went after her. She stopped on the steps and turned to face him, her back to the attic door.

"I won't sit at that table and listen to you find fault with everything Mom has done." Her words trembled and broke, but she didn't back down. "Who are you to find fault with Mom's judgment? You weren't here to pick a garden spot nor to work in it. She's had it all to do."

Julie wiped angrily at her tears, but she was determined to have her say if it killed her. "I have seen Mom do the work of a man and his horse to raise that garden. If she wants to bless and use those puny potatoes, that's her privilege."

The light from the coal-oil lamp cast flickering shadows around the two of them. She was small and dark, and he a threatening giant towering over her. Supper was forgotten as we sat silent and big-eyed, watching the two on the steps. Mom made a motion as if to rise, then sank back in her chair, and covered her face with her hands, as if she couldn't bear to look.

I thought Dad surely would kill Julie for defying him. I'd never known him to raise his hand to Mom or ever to hit Julie, but this was different. This was the first time one of his children had dared to stand up to him. Mom didn't often talk back to Dad or argue with him. And now Julie was talking to him just the way she did to one of us kids when we got out of line.

Dad lifted his hand and shook his finger in her face, but he didn't strike her. "Don't you dare to sass me, young lady! You're not so big that I can't turn you across my knee."

Where the light caught Dad's face, it looked red and swollen with held-in anger. Yet, when Julie stepped down as if to move away from him, he put his arm across her path and said quietly, "Look, girl, I . . ."

"You look!" she shouted. "You never see Mom and us kids any more."

She slipped by his upraised arm and ran out the door. He followed at her heels, swearing under his breath with every step he took. When Julie passed through the gate, she swung it shut so hard a loose paling fell, striking Dad on the shinbone.

He bent and picked it up, then stood slapping it against his leg while he looked down the road after her. We watched until Julie faded into the shadows and we couldn't see her any longer.

Our Fourth of July that had started out to be such a good day had ended with harsh words and bitterness. Julie was alone out there somewhere in the dark. And downstairs, Mom and Dad raised their voices to each other.

I cried myself to sleep. In the bed on the other side of the room, Jamie had nightmares and groaned in his sleep. All the grief and sorrow of the world seemed to have settled in our attic room.

I never knew when Julie slipped quietly into bed with me nor heard her get up the next morning; but when I went downstairs for breakfast, Julie was in the kitchen with Mom. They were both ready for church.

Dad was gone. I didn't ask where he was; it was enough just to know he wasn't there. Maybe it wasn't all his fault, but when he wasn't around, we were sure of peace and quiet. It would be two, maybe three or four weeks before he ran out of clean clothes and came home again.

Mom said, "Seely, get your brothers up for church and dress yourself. The others will have gone on without us if we don't hurry."

It was as if the night before had never happened. Just another bad dream to think on, then tuck away and forget. Mom never mentioned it. And if Julie spoke of it, Mom ignored her and changed the subject.

chapter ten

Not long afterward, the mining people came into the hills with big Mack trucks and bulldozers, just as Jase Perry had said they would. We had something new to think about.

Jamie and I watched from a distance as they tramped through the forest slashing and marking the big trees they could use for crossties and props in the mines.

The same trucks that moved the machines into the hills brought Ben Collier and his sawmill and set it up in the hollow about a mile from the gravel road. When the huge trees were cut and trimmed, they were hauled off in trucks or dragged with chains and pulleys to Ben Collier's sawmill.

I didn't like the noisy mill or the loud, groaning trucks and machinery that tore and ripped the hills and ruined the woods. "If these trucks keep going," I told Jamie, "we'll have to stay in the yard near our house. There won't be any place left in the woods to run and play."

Jamie said, "They had to put the mill there. It's the only flat, level place with a dirt road leading to it, except the schoolyard."

The way I felt about that schoolhouse, I thought that would have been the ideal place for them to put the sawmill. And I told Jamie so.

He looked at me as if I had suddenly sprouted horns and long pointed ears. "Why, Seely, where would we go to school if they did that?"

We wandered through the hills to the ridge above the big white house to see if anyone had moved into it. When we topped the rise, we saw smoke coming from the chimney and people walking in the yard. We lay belly down on the ground and parted the high tickle-grass so we could spy on them and not be seen.

While we watched, Ben Collier moved away from the others and went into the house. We heard the woman call to the boy and girl but not what she said to them. As they passed from sight around the corner of the big house, Jamie and I got to our feet and followed the path we'd made back to the sawmill.

I didn't say a word on the way back. I was too busy figuring out how to get acquainted with the blond Collier girl. She was about my size and looked to be about my age. She would have to go to our school—it was the only one anywhere near—and I would see her there. But I hated to waste the month or more until school started. I thought maybe she would come to her dad's mill and we would see her there, but only the boy came to work with his dad.

We saw the first fallen trees slide down the ground chute and watched as the big circle saw sliced the logs into long, rough boards as thin as a shingle. The men didn't pay any attention to us, and nobody said we couldn't hang around and watch them. Every day, we went by the sawmill to see if it was still standing and if the men were still working there.

When we tired of listening to the singing blade and counting the rough boards as they slid past it, we climbed the hills to the ridge above the Colliers' house and spied down the slope on them. We never once went down to the house or spoke to the kids. In the short time we had lived here, we had grown as shy and backward as the kids who had been born in the hills and never been beyond them.

Sometimes we would dare each other to call out to the yellow-haired girl while she walked alone in the yard, but we could never quite bring ourselves to yell loud enough for her to hear us.

It didn't take long after the trees were cut down for the tall sprouts and sucker limbs to grow thick around the raw edge of the stump, leaving plenty of room inside for a cool, shaded playhouse. We found one about four feet wide near the path leading toward the abandoned house where Jase and Dicie Perry and their kids had lived.

We would sit for hours on the tree stump in plain sight

of the Perry place, telling each other ghost stories. We never went any nearer the place and we always sat facing the house. Late in the afternoon when the sun filtered down through the trees making long, wavy shadows around us was the best time for telling stories, but it didn't leave us much time to get home before dark.

Jamie could tell better ghost stories than I, but I could scare him to tears with my tales about the long-dead Indians who had lived in these woods.

One day, when we were telling ghost stories, we heard people—live ones—coming up our path.

"Shut up!" Jamie told me. "Be quiet until we can see who it is."

We held our breath as the blond girl and her brother walked by our hideout. They were speaking in whispers and walking so softly their feet barely touched the ground. Soon after they passed us, they left the path and struck off through the woods toward their dad's mill.

"We missed our chance to talk to them," I told Jamie. "We should have called out to them as they walked by us."

"Couldn't you tell they were scared half to death, Seely?" Jamie said. "If we'd moved or called out to them, they never would've stopped running." After a moment's thought, he added, "Besides, they would have hated us forever for scaring them."

I had forgotten how it had been the first time Jamie and I had walked home through these woods. That day, we would've bolted and run at the slightest sound. But now, the woods were as familiar as our own back yard, and it was hard for me to imagine anyone being afraid of them.

It was just a few days later that Dad came home again. It had been nearly a month since his last time home. I guess he ran out of clean clothes or else he figured Mom was about out of money. He piled his dirty clothes in a stack on the kitchen floor and laid a bunch of money on the table.

Mom kind of laughed and said she felt like she was taking in washing and getting paid in advance for the work. She and Dad acted like they had forgotten what had happened the last time he was home.

But I could tell Julie hadn't forgotten. As soon as she saw Dad, she went upstairs to our bedroom. When I went up to tell her supper was ready, come and eat, she was writing a letter to Floyd Perry.

Floyd had gone into the three C's as soon as he could after Jase had killed himself and Dicie had been sent to the insane asylum over at Richmond. He'd written to Dad that he couldn't get a job, and he wasn't helping his mom and the little girls by mooning around the house all day. The last time he wrote to Dad he was somewhere in Idaho and was sending his checks to his grandma for the little girls' keep.

Floyd had written to Julie almost every week. She had bought ten cents' worth of penny postcards from the mailman and sent little notes back to him.

Then one night Dad had picked up and opened one of Floyd's letters to Julie before she found it, and he read it out loud at the supper table. I don't know why she got so angry about it. The letter didn't say much. Just that he couldn't make any plans for his future while he was taking care of his whole family.

When Dad handed the letter over to Julie, she wadded it up in a ball and threw it on the live coals in the cookstove.

The next morning Julie told Mom that Dad had no right to open her mail. She was entitled to a little privacy.

"Your daddy meant no harm by it," Mom told her. "He looks on Floyd Perry like one of his own."

"But he's not!" Julie flared out at Mom.

Although I hadn't seen any more of his letters, I guess Floyd had kept on writing to Julie because she wrote to him faithfully.

"Julie, Mom said for you to come to the table," I repeated.

"I heard you," she said.

"Well, come on!"

Reluctantly, she put the pencil and paper away and went down to the supper table. Dad didn't speak directly to Julie, or she to him. Mostly they acted as if the other one wasn't there.

When Dad left the house to walk over to the sawmill to talk to Ben Collier, Mom told Julie that she was just as stubborn and hard-headed as her dad. Neither one of them would give an inch in any direction.

"Maybe so," Julie said. "But I won't stay in the same room with him."

"We'll see about that," Mom said. And I guess she did.

93

Because Julie sat at the table and kept the peace until Dad went back to Crowe.

Before he left, Dad told Mom he wouldn't be home again before Labor Day. But if she'd make a list for him, he'd bring our school shoes and other things we needed when he came.

Usually Jamie and I would have been counting the days and couldn't wait until our new school things came, and we could start back to school again. But Jamie didn't seem to care this year. He had dark smudges under his eyes and cried easily. I don't think he was getting a full night's sleep often. I could hear him tossing and turning in his bed across the room from me. Sometimes he called out in his sleep and never knew when I answered him.

Mom said he'd worn himself out running all over the hills and hollows from daylight till dark. So we stopped going to the sawmill or over the ridge to spy on the Collier place. Seemed like every time we'd leave our yard, Mom called us back to the house.

On the days when I went to help Clara, Mom kept Jamie close to her so she could keep an eye on him.

chapter eleven

I was at Clara's on the Friday afternoon that Dad came home for the Labor Day weekend. By the time I got there, the school things he brought had been sorted out. On the bed I shared with Julie, tablets, pencils, ink, and pen were stacked on top of my school shoes. I cracked the back of the yellow tablet and wrote my name on the first line. Then I ran downstairs to see Jamie and Robert's new things. Even though Robert wouldn't be going to school, he got the same as Jamie. Just as Julie and I always got the same.

Jamie had a new jacket with a zipper, and he was trying it on for fit. He had never worked a zipper before, and he was having trouble getting the jacket to close.

"Let me do it, Jamie," I said. "I'll fasten it for you."

"Leave the boy alone," Dad said. "Let him do it for himself."

I stepped away from Jamie but stood waiting, ready to help him if he asked.

He quit trying to fasten the jacket and took it off. His face was pale and his hands trembled as he hung it up. Dad said I was making a sissy out of Jamie. He told Mom if she ever expected him to be a man or act like one, she'd better start treating him like one. He scuffled with Jamie and roughed him up until he ran crying out of the house.

When I would have gone after him, Dad said, "Leave him be!"

I ran out of the house anyhow and didn't stop running until I was in the cave under the big rock. There, in my notebook, I wrote down all my mixed-up feelings about Dad and wondered why it hurt so bad. Why did he have to come home? He didn't care about us, or he wouldn't do the things he did. He made Mom unhappy and fought with Julie, and now he'd hurt Jamie and made him cry. I hated him. I wished he would go back to Crowe and never come home.

At the supper table Jamie barely touched his food and excused himself as soon as I did, following me up the steps to our bedroom.

Julie went to Nancy Ann's early Saturday morning. Nancy Ann's mother had a dress shop in her home, and Julie had been helping her there every Saturday. She spent nearly every weekend at her house.

The morning was cool and overcast, so Jamie and I played in our room and wrote in our new yellow tablets.

After lunch, we went outside. Dad was working on the fence in front of the house, so we started around to the backyard.

"I've fixed the hinges on that gate and oiled them," Dad said. "And replaced the missing palings. So you kids watch how you use it."

We walked over to the gate and opened and closed it. Sure enough, it didn't squeak. I swung it back and forth a few times, testing it. "Don't swing on that gate!" We moved away from the gate and sat on the porch steps watching him.

He was fixing the picket fence out by the road when the mailman stopped and handed him a letter.

Dad turned it over in his hands, read the return address, then slowly tore the narrow end off the sealed envelope, took out the message, and read it. Then he returned the letter to the envelope and slipped it into the bib pocket of his overalls.

At the supper table he said to Mom, "Floyd Perry will probably be home any day now. He wrote Julie that any kind of a job would pay him better than the three C's."

Mom said, "Do you think a kid like that can even find a job nowadays?"

"I don't know," Dad replied. "Ben Collier was telling me just yesterday he could use a regular hand over at the sawmill. I thought I'd go over and speak to him tonight about giving Floyd the job. Floyd would make him a good, steady worker, if he hasn't found someone already."

Dad put the letter, addressed to Julie, on the stand table when he left for Crowe. She found it there when she got home later that Sunday. She picked it up, then threw it down again. She started to walk away, but turned back, and took the letter with her to the attic.

When Mom sent me to the attic to make the boys' bed and pick up things, Julie had my geography book spread across our bed, opened to the big map of the United States, and she was pencil-marking the shortest way home to Greene County from Idaho.

Dad came home the weekend school started, and the week after that. I heard him tell Mom that he'd try to get home every week and get the place ready for winter. After bad weather set in, he might not be able to make it home for two or three months.

I watched the clouds swinging low over the hills and waited impatiently for winter.

When school started, Doris and Carney Collier came to our school, but Doris was quiet and standoffish. The very first day, Frieda and I asked her to come play with us, but she just shook her head and turned away.

She always got to school just in time to take her seat before the bell rang and was the first one to leave the room when school was out.

Doris wore two or three different dresses that first week. They were always starched slick and hardly faded at all. I thought she felt like she was too good to play with us because we had only one or two dresses to our names, and they had been washed and faded until they hung limply around our knees.

Dad said he bet Ben Collier made a good living from his sawmill. He ought to; if he didn't, he wasn't out any money for hired hands. Most of his help were men working off a debt for raw slab lumber. All of them but Floyd Perry. He said Ben was lucky to get Floyd for any amount of money.

Floyd had come to our house the first week after school started. He was a lot bigger than when he went away. He slung the canvas bag that held all his stuff into a corner of the kitchen and lifted Mom plumb off her feet in a bear hug. Her eyes had been wet when he finally put her down.

Then he had turned and gathered the boys up in his arms and smiled at Julie over their heads. Floyd slept on a pallet on the kitchen floor that night and set off early in the morning to see Ben at the mill. He went to work for Ben that morning and got a room with board at the teacher's house.

Floyd didn't come over often, he was kept too busy working at the mill. He said people came from all over the county and bought the rough planks and built houses. Or they would build on another room or porch to the house they lived in. Dad said the lumber was green and unseasoned. It would warp all out of shape in a year's time. A man was a fool or worse, who would waste his time and money building a house with green boards.

I thought a warped barn and porch would be better than the ones we had, but, wisely, I never said so. Every time the wind came up, I expected to see our porch go flying through the air. The holes and loose boards had to be skirted like a game of hop-scotch whenever we used the front door. But if Dad said a hole in the floor was better than a solid, warped board, I'd better believe it, even if I fell through the hole.

I supposed that was the reason Doris wouldn't have anything to do with Frieda and me. She lived in a big house with a solid porch, and her papa made a lot of money at the sawmill.

Doris was a small-boned girl with long yellow hair and the bluest eyes. Not deep blue like the violets that bloomed thick in the woods, but blue like the skies in summer. Her skin was so pale and thin I could see every vein like fine blue threads on a white quilt top. When she bent forward over her desk, her hair covered her face, and all I could see was her starched dress and fine dandelion hair. She reminded me of an ear of unshucked corn, its bright silk tassel sprouting from one end. I thought the reason she sat in the room and read during the noon hour was probably because she was too frail to mix in our games and would break into a million pieces if she ever fell.

Last year Frieda and I had sat together at noon and traded sandwiches. But this year she walked home for her lunch every day. Her mother was expecting a baby, and Frieda had to help her. She lived a ways from school and sometimes she barely made it back before the bell rang. I sat on one side of the school room to eat lunch and Doris sat on the other.

Sometimes, when I would glance her way, I would surprise her looking in my direction. But she never smiled or even acted like she saw me. She would quick drop her head or look out the window next to her desk.

Maybe, if we had gone down to her house just once last summer, Doris and I would be friends right now. I wished Jamie and I had leaped from our hiding place in the woods that day and made ourselves known to her and Carney. Even if it had scared them, they would've been over it by now.

The boys yelled, "Stuck-up! Stuck-up! Hair like a buttercup." But Doris sat quietly at her desk and read, as if she was the only one in the room and hadn't heard a word they said.

Then one day while we sat reading with an empty room between us. Doris asked to borrow the book I had when I was finished with it.

I said, "Sure, if you like Gene Stratton Porter's books. This one is about a girl named Amaryllis who lives in a magic garden."

She smiled at me. "I know. I read a lot of her books. Whenever I can find one."

From then on, we exchanged books, helped each other on book reports for English class, and swapped our family history.

She had an older sister. But her sister Della was a lot older than Julie and had been out of school a long time. Doris said Della had worked in the city until she began to get fat, then she quit her job and came home to stay.

She said, "Della hardly ever leaves the house. Papa built a room onto the big house for her, and she stays in there most of the time. Della doesn't like living back in the hills, but Mama told her it wasn't what she liked that made her fat, but what she got. So she never says much about it anymore."

As the days grew shorter, the noon hours seemed to grow shorter. Our class assignments became easier when Doris and I did them together. We whispered and giggled as we bent our heads over the huge encyclopedia to look up assignments for history. We both hated that class, but together we made it fun instead of a distasteful task.

We found out we were the same age, liked a lot of the same things, and disliked some people for the same reasons. We talked a lot, but she didn't say much more about her family or where they had lived before they moved to Greene County. I didn't ask her any questions. I figured if she wanted me to know about it, she would tell me.

She seemed to be starved for someone to talk to and as eager as I was to be friends. I wondered how I could have thought her stuck-up. She was nice.

chapter twelve

Doris was in the eighth grade with Frieda and me. Carney was older than Doris but a grade behind her in school. He wasn't dim-witted or stupid; he just wasn't interested. Doris said that once her papa had sworn Carney was going to get an education and amount to something if it killed the both of them. From the way it looked to me, most likely it would.

One evening, Doris asked me to walk home with her. The day was cloudy and overcast, and dusk had fallen earlier than usual. The hills with their tall trees and dark thickets of hazelnut frightened her. She had lived in the hills all fall and part of the summer, but her mama made her stay close to home.

"I guess if it wasn't for school," Doris said, "she'd never let me out of her sight."

I wanted to tell her that Jamie and I had spied on her and watched her house from the top of the ridge that summer, but I wasn't sure she would understand. Our friendship was too new, and the thought of losing her for a friend scared me to death.

Doris always stayed after school now and helped me clean the room. Since Frieda had got her new baby brother and had to hurry home every day, I had been doing it alone. Every night I'd walk home with Doris when we'd finished and cut back above the sawmill on the path Jamie and I had made over the ridge and through the woods. I would still get home about the same time, so no one knew I took Doris home; and I didn't tell them.

One evening when we were done earlier than usual, I took Doris down the path that led to our house. At the footlog I told her, "If you ever want to come to my house, just cross the creek there, and when you get to the top of the bank on the other side, you can see our barn. Jamie and I have made a clear path from the barn to the footlog and up to our hidden cave."

I pointed to the big flat rock that jutted out from the hillside. The trees that had shielded it from sight all summer were nearly bare, and the rock stood out in plain view for all to see. I had never taken Frieda to the cave, but now I said to Doris, "Would you like to see my secret place? No one else knows about it but Jamie. We share it. But he won't mind if I share it with you."

She came eagerly, kicking the yellow and red beech

and maple leaves that lay thick on the ground as she walked. The smoky purple haze of Indian summer still hovered over the hills, but dusk had already settled in the room under the big flat rock.

Doris hesitated at the mouth of the cave, then ducked her head and followed me into the deep shadows of the place Jamie and I claimed for our own.

No matter how hard or how long it rained, the space under the rock was always dry. The stone ledge where Jamie set his cigar box of treasures never drew dampness or mildew.

I showed Doris where I kept my diary notebook stuck in a crack between the rocks. The pages were coming loose from the backstitching, and I had to watch how I handled it. The notebook was nearly full except for a few empty lines and blank places that I was saving in case something important happened. I wanted to be sure I had a place to write it all down.

When I pulled the notebook from between the rocks to show Doris how dry the cave stayed all the time, loose pages fell from my hand and scattered across the dirt floor. She picked them up and stepped toward the light.

"It's my diary," I said quickly, and moved to take them from her hands.

She looked up from the paper she was reading and said, "Oh, but it's about this cave. Only you make it sound like Ali Baba's cave and not just a hollow place in the hill, like it really is."

I dropped my hands and stepped back. I was half angry—and so ashamed I couldn't look at her. Now she would know that I not only told stories, I even wrote them down to keep like some treasure. I wished with all my heart the floor would crack open and swallow me from sight.

"Tomorrow," I promised myself, "I'll tear it all in tiny pieces and throw it in Lick Crick where no one else can ever read it."

Then Doris spoke again. "Seely, I won't read anymore if you don't want me to; and I won't tell your secret to a soul. Cross my heart and hope to die. My mama thinks I'm lazy and selfish because I like to be by myself and draw pictures. I don't have any place to keep my pictures and Mama throws them away. She says I'm wasting my time. But I've got lots of time. I just start all over again on another piece of paper."

Suddenly, I felt all right again. "My mom says it's a disgrace the way I tell lies," I told Doris. "But it's not really lying. It's just seeing things the way you want them to be or telling the story different from the way it really happened to make it funny and happy."

I dug along the wall beside Jamie's rock ledge and cleared the dirt away, leaving a clean, smooth surface.

"You can have this end for your stuff if you want to share our hideaway," I said. "Jamie won't care. He likes you, too."

The next day Doris had her schoolbag loaded with brown wrapping paper and big black marking pencils from her papa's mill. After we finished cleaning the school, we stopped by the cave again and stored her belongings before going on to her house.

Doris asked me one night if I had hair under my arms or between my legs.

I said, "No. Why should I have hair under my arms or anywhere else?"

"I don't either," she replied. "But we've got to be real careful once hair starts growing there."

She walked a little farther, kicking at the dead leaves and twigs lying in the path. She stopped and waited for me to catch up to her. "You tell me if you see any hair growing on your body any place, and I'll be sure to tell you. I don't know why we get all hairy, but when we do, we can have babies real easy if we aren't careful."

I thought about what she had told me all the way home. I couldn't understand how one thing could have anything to do with the other. But I was sure going to watch for signs of hair.

Instead of Doris having the answers to the questions that were puzzling me, she had given me another problem to fret over.

It was raining when Doris came to my house for the first time on a Saturday. We had to stay indoors all day. Mom didn't like it, but she never said a word about it. Instead she went about the house tight-lipped and banging cabinet doors and pots and pans, as if they were at fault and the cause of the rain.

The rain didn't let up until late in the evening. We were eating supper when Carney knocked on the kitchen door and said his mama had sent him over to get Doris and walk home with her. Mom didn't ask him to sit down, nor did she ask them to come back again when they left.

After they had gone and Mom knew they couldn't hear her, she started to preach at me. "You don't need to think for one minute, young lady, that you're going to start running around with Doris Collier. I don't want her in this house, or to ever hear tell of you going over there."

"Why ever not? I like Doris. Her mama says I can stay all night with her anytime I want to. And I want to Monday night. I've already promised."

"Don't you sass me, Missy! You heard what I said. That girl will turn out to be just like her sister, Della. Fat with a big belly, and more than likely, she don't even know who it was that got her that way. Now, you shut up about it."

I shut up, but I didn't stop thinking about what she had said. Doris was as skinny as a broom. She would never be as fat as Della.

chapter thirteen

Monday night I sent a note home with Jamie to say I was going home with Doris to stay all night. He took the slip of yellow paper, folded it, and put it in his pocket.

"Does Mom know you're going to stay with Doris tonight?"

I crossed my fingers behind my back. "Yes. She knows it."

I knew it was a far cry from Mom knowing I wanted to go and her saying I could, but I was ready to risk her anger this once. I wanted to see what it was like to sleep away from home. I never had, and Julie got to all the time.

Doris and I took our own sweet time cleaning the school room. We used the last of the water to wash and scrub the brown scum from the inside walls of the big water crock. We filled the jug with fresh water every day, but it looked like no one had ever cleaned it. When we had finished, it took both of us to carry the jug outside to dump the dirty water and to lift it back on to the table when we were done with it.

It was after dusk when we locked the door and started down the path to her house. Doris took my hand and held tight as we approached the dark woods. She kept glancing back over her shoulder as if she expected something to creep up behind and grab her.

"I'm not really afraid of these woods when you're walking with me. But sometimes, when I'm alone, I think I hear footsteps like someone following me. Then, when I stop and look back, there isn't a soul on the path. One time, I thought I saw Simmy Walters hiding behind some trees. But maybe he was just going by here on his way to town."

I said, "Simmy Walters? Frieda's uncle? What on earth would he be doing on the path to your house? He doesn't live around here."

Simmy wasn't as old as my dad or Mr. Thompson, but I'd bet he was thirty. I couldn't imagine what he would be doing in our part of the woods. He hardly ever went to Frieda's. She told me he only came by once in awhile for a good meal and a place to sleep. I didn't know Doris had ever seen or heard tell of Simmy. I'd only seen him once.

Doris said, "He used to hang around with Della. But lately, he's sure made himself scarce around our house."

She peered into the darkening woods as if she expected Simmy to jump out in front of her. "Papa says he'll shoot his backside off if he ever dares to show his face at our house again."

I giggled, and the sober expression fled from Doris's face. She laughed and the scar on the left side of her face deepened into a wide dimple. I had asked her once how she had got the scar, and she said, "It was my uncle Mac's fault. He left his razor on the table and I tried to shave and cut my face."

That was the only time I ever heard Doris mention any family except the ones she lived with. I had thought she was like me and didn't have any relatives, just dead ancestors.

Doris and I went directly upstairs when we got to her house. There were four bedrooms up there, with doors opening off a wide hall. She and her mama had the two rooms on one side of the hall, and her papa and Carney slept on the other side. Della had the big room which had been built on downstairs. Even before we moved to Greene County, we never had that many rooms.

Doris couldn't believe it when I told her my mom and dad slept together in the same room, and I had shared a bed with Julie all my life.

After she had changed from her school skirt to a cotton dress, we went down to the living room. I told Doris I bet we could've set our whole house into that one room. She laughed and said she bet I would bet on anything. I said, "Well, I'll bet you've got the biggest house in the county."

We looked through the books that were shelved along one wall and took down a heavy encyclopedia. We carried it to a table in the middle of the room and began to turn the pages. Then it dawned on me. They didn't have a stove! Everybody we knew had a stove in the middle of their front room. But the Colliers didn't.

"Hey, where's the heating stove? How do you keep it warm in here?"

Doris said, "There's a furnace in the cellar under the house. It heats all the rooms, except Della's. She has a stove in there. Papa built it after we moved here and it doesn't have a cellar."

Della's room had been built of rough lumber and stained a deep walnut on the outside. It had a shake shingle roof that joined the eaves of the kitchen and came down to the ground on the far end. There was a wide plank door opening onto a porch, which ran the full length of the room, and a boardwalk leading to the privy.

Ben had built the privy, too. A sizable three-holer that set downhill from their well and downwind from the house. Doris and I were perched over the high seats when we heard her mama calling us to supper. We ran up hill all the way to the house and didn't get our breath until we were seated at the round oak table.

I sat next to Doris and faced Carney across the table. I bowed my head waiting for someone to give thanks. When no one spoke, I looked up. Carney winked at me and made a face. His mama said, "Carney," quietly. And I bent my head, again.

Carney's voice rolled out like he was calling hogs from

forty miles downstream. "Good food, good meat, good Lord, let's eat."

I forgot to keep my eyes closed and my head down. I stared at him until he finished speaking, then he winked again and stuck out his tongue at me.

Ben laughed and passed the meat platter to Carney. I kept my eyes on my plate and didn't look at him once all during supper.

Della left the table while the rest of us were still eating. When she stood to leave the table, she smiled shyly at me, and I thought how beautiful she was with her wide dark eyes and all that shining black hair framing her small, pale face.

She was fatter than she had been the last time I had seen her. Her stomach was bulging out where her legs met at her straddle and lay in her lap like a large, hard pumpkin when she sat down. She walked funny, too, like a woman carrying a heavy basket of wet wash out to the clothes line. As I watched her walk from the room, I thought, "Why, she looks just like Mom did before Robert came, like she's expecting a baby!" But how could that be? Della didn't have a husband.

Mrs. Collier left the table right after Della and followed her to her room and shut the door.

Doris and I did the dishes. She washed, I wiped, and we both put them away. Each dish had its place in the cabinet, and the shelves had clean white paper on them. Mom saved newspaper to line our cabinet drawers and shelves. I just supposed everyone did. But the white paper did look cleaner and prettier.

Mrs. Collier came out of Della's room and told us to take a lamp and go upstairs. We could do our homework up there. She said Della wasn't feeling well and our talking and giggling were disturbing her.

I had been sound asleep when the screaming woke me. I was still curled to Doris's back, the way we had gone to sleep.

Her hands were over her ears, and she was trembling and shaking, trying to muffle the sound of her crying.

I whispered, "Sh-sh-sh, it's only the hoot owls. A hoot owl nearly scared me to death, the first time I ever heard one scream. But they won't hurt you."

The next scream sounded nearer, like it was right in this house with us. I wondered if hoot owls could get in our room and what I could do if they did.

Doris turned to me and put her wet face against my shoulder. I smoothed her hair with one hand and patted her back with the other, just the way I did Jamie when he had one of his fits. I patted her and talked to her until she quieted her crying. I could tell by her breathing that she had gone back to sleep.

I couldn't go to sleep, but I didn't hear any more screaming. I heard footsteps in the kitchen, though, and the sound of metal touching metal with a soft clanging together. It reminded me of the ghost stories Jamie told. There was always a skeleton dragging a chain across the floor or up and down the stairs, in all of them.

I moved closer to Doris and listened to the creaking boards in the floor downstairs. Once, I heard a door open and close and someone walking on Della's porch. As I was drifting off to sleep, someone came upstairs, footsteps passed in the hall, and a door closed at the far end.

My last thought was that Carney had been trying to scare Doris and me with all those weird noises.

Mrs. Collier shook me awake. "You girls are late for school. Get up, and be quiet getting dressed. There's no time for breakfast. Now, you both hurry!"

My arms were numb where Doris had slept on them. My fingers tingled and I had trouble tying my shoes. I broke a shoestring, but we both broke all records getting dressed and ready for school. Carney was nowhere around as we grabbed our books and left the house, running for the woods and the short cut to school. We were in the clearing when the first bell rang and walked through the door as class was called to order.

I didn't learn much in school that day. My mind was on the night just passed and the one coming on. I would have to face up to Mom for going against her word. I hoped for a switching. It wouldn't last as long as a tongue-lashing nor hurt half as much. I wished with all my heart I hadn't gone near the Colliers. I wished it was tomorrow. Lord, I wished I was dead!

Doris left as soon as the dismissal bell rang. She was the first one out the door and walking fast, as if she couldn't wait to get home. I cleaned up half-heartedly and then I just poked along home. I could wait.

I sat at the supper table, my eyes glued to the plate of cold bacon and pancakes, my dry mouth chewing up food I couldn't swallow. Mom was giving me old billy-hell for going home with Doris. Every word she spoke was worse than a hickory stick across my back, and I knew I had it coming for disobeying her.

"I'll swear I don't know what I'm going to do with you, Seely. You won't mind a word I say to you. I'll let your daddy take care of you when he gets home."

I thought, "It's nearly over, thank God."

Whenever Mom said she would let Dad handle something or other, it meant she had washed her hands of the whole kit and caboodle. More than likely this would be the last I ever heard of it. She would never mention it to Dad. If he knew, it would be like stirring up a hornet's nest with a fiery stick.

The next morning I met Doris where the rail fence marked the boundary of the playground. She linked her arm through mine, and we walked together to the door. We both talked at once, hearing but not listening to what the other one was saying.

"Papa hadn't left for the mill, yet. Usually, when he and Mama are fussing, he gets up early and leaves for work. But not today. Mama got testy about Papa's tools on the kitchen table last night. Papa said she shouldn't be so touchy about where he left the tools of his trade. A man's trade was his woman's living. Then Mama told him to get her living off the table, she didn't want to look at it."

I laughed. Doris went on with her story.

"I don't think it's the tools they're fighting about. Mama's using them as an excuse to cover something else. Papa said, 'You were plenty pleased to see me dump them there last night.' Mama looked up and saw me and said, 'Shush, we'll not talk about it now.' I'll bet they could hardly wait for me to get out of earshot."

The last bell rang as we hurried to our seats.

chapter fourteen

*T*he dried brown corn-
stalks were higher than my head. Dead leaves rattled and
cracked in the cold wind, like skeleton bones, as I followed the path I had made last summer through the
green corn. This was the first time I'd been in the cornfield since the corn had been husked. I felt as if I was
walking through a forest of cornstalks. Wherever I
looked, all I could see were the tall brown stalks and gold
leaves waving in the cold wind. I thought how easy it
would be to get lost in this skeleton forest. I would just
let my feet wander in any row they happened to stumble
onto and not even look at the path. I had tried once to get
lost in the fog on the way to school, but somehow my
feet had found the way to the schoolhouse door.

The only sound was the crackling corn leaves above
my head. I was cold and wishing I had never promised

Clara to go with her today. I thought of all the other things I could be doing as I zigzagged my way down the narrow path.

The path ended behind the Brent barn, near the wood-pile. I could see George cutting hickory bark for stove kindling and hear Clara calling from the house. He didn't seem to hear her, and I know he didn't hear me. He was talking to himself.

"Guess if I was dead and in hell with my back broke, I'd still hear that damn fool woman hollering, 'More bark, George. Come and put a stick of wood in the stove, George!' Helpless damn fool woman."

He must have seen my shadow fall across the wood-pile. He stopped talking to himself and turned around.

"Hi there, little one. You want to see Clara? She's in the kitchen. Go right on in, she'll be right glad to see you."

I walked toward the back door, kicking at a few wood chips and looking at the worn, scuffed toes of my shoes. I hoped Clara would be "right glad" to see me. Maybe she had changed her mind or forgotten she'd asked me to go to the city with her.

I was uncomfortable about going to the county seat with Clara. When she asked Mom if I could keep her company on the drive, Mom said it would be good for me. I was always a little leery of anything Mom said was good for me. They were usually things like castor oil, spinach, and turnip greens.

Clara Brent was drying the breakfast dishes and putting them in the glass-front cabinet when I knocked on the door and then walked in without waiting. Most of the women didn't like it when the kids did that, but Clara didn't mind one whit. She said it saved her the trouble of walking to the door. I could see why she wouldn't want to walk any more than she had to. Her tiny feet and ankles didn't look hardly strong enough to carry all the weight she piled on them.

She said she was glad for my company on the trip to the county seat. George wasn't any fit companion on a drive of any kind, she told me. She told me a lot of things that George wasn't.

Clara drove right down the middle of the road, swerving to one side when we met another car, then back to the middle again. She chatted and asked questions all the while about everybody I knew. Usually, she just kept on talking and didn't give me a chance to answer her. But when she asked me if Della Collier's baby was a boy or a girl, she paused and didn't go on, waiting for me to tell her.

I must have resembled a tongue-tied imbecile, because Clara said, "You mean you don't know? Or ain't she had it yet? It was due ten days or two weeks ago."

So that was the reason why Della was so fat. She *was* going to have a baby. "But she doesn't have a husband!" I'd blurted my thoughts out loud.

Clara turned her head to look at me and ran off the edge of the gravel road. She got the car back in the middle of the road before she said, "Didn't anyone ever tell you, Seely, that a husband isn't necessary for a girl to have a baby?"

We didn't talk about having babies at our house. Babies came, they were there, and we accepted them. It seemed to me, they grew overnight. One day, a family wouldn't have a baby, then the very next day there was a baby in the house. But there was always a husband there first.

Clara gave me an odd look from the corner of her eye and didn't say anything more about Della. We were coming into the city limits, and I guess she had to pay attention to her driving. It was just a little after ten, but already the streets were packed with people who had come to town to do their Saturday trading. Clara dodged the oncoming traffic and the cars parked along the street, until she came to the courthouse. She parked haphazardly in two spaces on the town square, took me by the hand, and struck off catty-cornered across the street.

"You've been so good to help me all summer," she said, "and then with the canning this fall. I'd like to get you a few things. I don't know what you kids hanker for nowadays, so you come along with me and pick out what you want."

I told her I hadn't done anything. It was the truth. I had been at her house when she was canning, but I just watched her and listened to her stories, the same as I had been doing all summer long.

She said it was time I learned to pick out my clothes and buy wisely. A girl was never too young to learn how to spend money. She chuckled and pulled me into a store.

I was taken by the soft lavender color of a skirt and blouse in the window. But Clara rummaged through a load of dresses on a long iron rack and pulled a horrible mustard-colored one with long sleeves from a hanger and held it up to me. I slumped so it would hang long. She put it back on the rack and picked out another. I stood there shaking my head at every dress she showed me.

Finally, she said, "Seely, what do you think?" I pointed to the lavender skirt and blouse in the window. Clara liked them, too, and she bought them. She bought me three pairs of cotton-knit panties, as well, which made a change for every school day, if I counted the two pairs Mom had made me from feed sacks. I always had one pair on and one pair drying.

I tried on one pair of shoes after the other to find a pair that didn't squeeze my feet. Dad always bought my shoes, and they would pinch and burn my toes till they fell off my feet. One year, I had worn the shoes he bought for Jamie. They were wide, square-toed, and thick-soled and didn't touch my feet any place. The kids at school had laughed at me for wearing a boy's shoes, but I had worn them anyway and pretended I didn't know what they were laughing about.

When we'd finished shopping, Clara headed for the café whose rusty sign screeched and whined in the wind. Inside, steam covered the windows and soaked the fly-specked menu pasted on the inside glass. The smell of coffee and bacon frying made my mouth water.

Clara headed for a booth at the back of the room. With the high sides around us, we couldn't see the other people, and no one could watch us eat.

She slid her tiny feet out of her high-heeled pumps

and rubbed her ankles together while we studied the grease-spotted menu propped against the wall.

Clara ordered for both of us. When the food came, I ate greedily. I was too hungry to be polite and wait for her. Peanut butter on cold biscuits would have tasted good to me right then, and I hated peanut butter above all things on earth.

"Honey, how old are you, now?" Mrs. Brent asked while we were eating.

I swallowed my mouthful of food. "I'll be twelve in December. Ten days from today, on Tuesday."

She cocked her head to one side and peered at me from under the folds of her eyelids. I wondered if she could see the two stubby horns beginning to show on my chest. She was staring in that direction.

I wore my shirts as loose as possible and slumped my shoulders when I thought of it to keep the bumps from showing. But the blouses were old, and I was outgrowing them before they wore out. Slumping didn't hide as much as I hoped it would.

"It's not going to be long, now, till you'll be needing some brassieres. I guess your mom hasn't noticed, but you're getting to be a young lady."

Clara took a bite of roll and chewed thoughtfully. "Have you started your periods yet?" she whispered.

I was squirming and trying to slump my shirt loose in front. My face was hot and I knew it must be red. The only periods I knew of came at the end of a sentence. I had never heard of having one. But just from the way she asked, I figured it had something to do with the bumps on my chest and the soft downy fuzz growing in my arm pits, but I wasn't sure. And until I could ask Doris about it, I wouldn't say anything. Not even to Clara.

She leaned across the table and patted my hand. "Well, never mind that now. It's late and we'd better be getting along toward home."

I slid out of the booth and gathered up my packages.

"My, what a lot of brought-on pretties you'll have to show off tonight."

Mom wasn't going to like it, I knew. She wouldn't allow us kids to take anything that had a tinge of charity, and these things would smack to high heaven of charity to her. I could just hear her now. "You'll not keep a stitch of that stuff, Missy. Don't need to harbor the thought for one second. If your daddy can't buy for you, you'll do without!" I hugged my packages closer to my chest.

Maybe Mom wouldn't notice me tonight, but wait till she saw me in these things tomorrow morning. That thought wiped the smile off my face in a hurry, and I walked a little slower down the street behind Clara.

chapter fifteen

*F*loyd worked at the sawmill for Ben from daylight to dark. He didn't have much time for fooling around, he told Julie, but sometimes he borrowed the teacher's car and took her in to McVille for a soda.

Mom watched them like a hawk. I could come and go as I pleased, like going to town with Clara, but Julie had to account for every minute she was out of Mom's sight. I would hear Mom questioning Julie when she came home from a ride in the car with Floyd, and Julie's irate answers.

Mom told her once she was going to end up just like Della Collier if she wasn't careful. Julie had answered angrily, "If I do, you'll have drove me to it!"

She never should have mentioned driving anywhere. Mom started in about the car again.

I wasn't sure I was going to like being a grown-up woman. But so far, I hadn't figured out how to keep from it. I would much rather stay the way I was and be eleven all the time.

Julie was grown-up, and there was one rule for the things she could do, and a lot of others on what she didn't dare do. If she didn't abide by them, Mom said she was courting hell's fire or, worse yet, an end like Della Collier's.

I got up early the Sunday morning after I'd been to town with Clara and put on the new lavender blouse and skirt and blue shoes before I went downstairs to breakfast. Mom took one look and nearly dropped the pan of biscuits she was taking from the oven. "Where on earth did you get that outlandish outfit?"

I started to tell her. "Mrs. Brent gave . . ."

"Well, you can give it back! There's no call for that woman to be buying your clothes."

"Here it comes," I thought. I could recite it word for word.

"If your daddy can't buy your dresses, you can do without. Now, change your clothes and call your brothers to breakfast."

I yelled from the foot of the stairs. "Jamie! Robert! Come and eat!" I didn't change my clothes.

Mom said, "I told you to wake your brothers, not the folks who live a mile down crick."

I ate with one eye on the clock and the other on the

back door. I wanted to be ready to grab my coat and leave for church the minute Doris and Frieda walked in the door.

Doris didn't have anything new for church, so we swapped blouses. I pulled her sailor middie over my head while she buttoned into my lavender one. Doris had stubby horns growing on her chest, also. I wondered if she hated them the way I did. She didn't slump or try to hide them. She acted as if she didn't know they were there. I hadn't thought about it before, but Frieda's blouse had always been full across the chest. Especially when she was wearing a sweater, like today.

In church that morning, Carney Collier sat behind us on the hard wooden bench saved for the latecomers. He poked Frieda in the back with his hymnbook and tried to talk to her when we stood for prayer. Finally, he slipped her a note written on a flyleaf torn from the hymnal.

The note said, "You're as pretty as a speckled pup. Will you walk home with me after church?"

We giggled when we read it, and a woman seated in front of us turned around and frowned and shook her head.

Carney walked with us to the dirt lane that angled off toward the mill. Frieda walked a few steps up the lane, talked for a moment, then came back to where Doris and I were waiting for her.

She said, "Carney's going to meet me here next Sunday and walk to church with us."

Big deal! Who would want to walk to church with

Carney? I hadn't forgotten how he had behaved the night I stayed at their house.

We teased Frieda about getting a beau in church. We said we bet the only reason she ever went was to see the boys.

She blushed and said, "Well, I'm not getting any younger, and I don't want to be an old maid."

"I'll probably be an old maid," Doris said. "I'd get skinned alive if I ever so much as looked at a boy."

"It's a sure bet that I'll die an old maid. I'd have to be skinned before a boy would ever look at me. Not that I'd want one to," I added.

Doris smiled and touched my face. "You'll be a pretty woman, Seely, when you grow up. You've got good bones."

I didn't want to have to go that far to be pretty. Doris was just trying to make me feel good. It was what grown-ups often said about people when they couldn't find anything else good to say. If I had to grow up, it was going to be for a better reason than that one.

But I did think God had slighted me, and I had told Him so in church. I had prayed and asked Him to please make my hair turn dark chestnut, like my mother's, and fall in deep waves to my shoulders, like Julie's; but it never changed. It still hung white and straight as a string, like the girl's hair on the Dutch cleanser can.

I was about ready to give up on prayers and wishes. It was just like Mom said, "Wish in one hand and blow in the other, you'll get the same thing."

Doris and I slipped quietly into Mom's bedroom to

change our blouses again and closed the door. I had my arms over my head, struggling to get out of the middie blouse, when I heard the door open. I turned my back as the footsteps came toward me, then I felt Mom's hands at the buttons, loosening the sleeves, and lifting the middie over my head. She turned it right side out, handed it to Doris, and passed the lavender blouse to me.

"If you're bound and determined to keep that outfit, you'd best take care of it. You know I don't hold with you loaning your things."

Doris was tugging at my hand, wanting to get out of the house. So did I, but Mom had a fold of my skirt in her hand, rubbing it between her thumb and finger.

"This feels like good material, soft to the touch but tight-woven." She dropped the skirt and stepped back. "Well, what are you girls standing around in here for? Go and play outside."

We raced out of the house, past the barn, across the footlog and into the woods. Laughing and breathless, we dropped on to the big, flat, overhanging rock to rest. During the past year, Jamie and I and the wind had worn the huge rock smooth and clean.

From up there, we could see the high banks where Lick Crick ran into the wide, muddy water of White River and far off, the sandy bottom land where watermelons grew round and juicy in the summertime.

The big rock was warm on the side where the sun had touched it, and the cold wind didn't strike us there. We sat close together on the warm stone and imagined we were flying the Atlantic with Amelia Earhart; we were well known public figures, dressed up in red satin and patent leather spike heels, having dinner at the White House. The President was at one end of the long table and Mrs. Roosevelt was at the other. Doris and I were seated right next to the President.

Then Doris said, "What are you eating tonight?"

I thought the play acting was finished. I said, "It's Sunday. Chicken and dumplings, for sure."

She rolled around on the rock, screaming with laughter. "I can just see President and Mrs. Roosevelt eating stewed chicken and dumplings for supper."

She was still laughing and wiping her eyes.

I turned away from her. "I don't care what they eat for supper. I was through playing that stupid old game, anyway."

The silence stretched between us. I felt chilled to the bone and wanted to move closer to Doris, but I hated to be the one to give in. I got up, walked around the top of the rock, and sat down as near as I could get to her. "Let's talk about Someday, Doris. All the things we're going to do Someday."

"You mean, when we grow up? I'm going to paint this hill country in every color of the rainbow. I'll be a very famous artist and probably die a tragic death before my time."

I said, "People don't die before their time. I know. Whenever somebody dies, Mom always says, 'Well, it was their time to go.'"

Another long, heavy silence settled around us. This time it was Doris who spoke first. "Oh, Seely, you're just being ornery. You know it was just pretend. I draw pictures because there's nothing else to do back here in the hills. It's all make-believe, like your fancy stories. We'll probably both end up like all the other hill women, with a pot of beans on the stove and ten kids underfoot."

We giggled and moved close together again on the big flat rock.

"Let's go to Frieda's house and see what she's doing. Maybe she has some scrap paper we can use. We've got all day for our drawing and writing, and here we sit, doing nothing."

Every time we went to see Frieda, Doris stayed in the yard and drew pictures of the dilapidated barn. I had thought at first she used her drawing as an excuse to keep from going into the house, but she truly thought the old falling down barn was beautiful.

She had stacks and stacks of sketches of the faded gray barn in the cave. She made drawings of the footlog on Lick Crick, too, with the weeping willows drooping along the bank, their branches trailing to the water's edge. Lately, she had been drawing the bare skeleton trees that stood on the hillside, the animal tracks winding down them like blood vessels on the back of a man's hand. In her pictures, the tracks all led to the river, and the river ran out of the hills.

Doris liked to draw pictures of me, too. While I sat quietly writing or reading, she would make pencil drawings of my long hands and solemn face. She would say, "Smile, Seely. You look so sad and stern when you're not smiling. No wonder the kids think you're mad all the time."

When Jamie tagged along with us, Doris would put our

two faces close together on the same piece of paper. Jamie always had a small, shy smile; and sometimes she would catch the soft, dreamy look in his eyes. Doris said we were like the two sides of a man's life. Jamie was the dreamer and planner of beautiful things and I the stern discipliner. In the pictures Doris gave to Mom, I could see a strong resemblance between my dad and me. I decided to look more closely at him the next time he came home.

I thought Jamie favored Mom. But I held my tongue. We had to keep him in good humor with us so we could use his school paper. Or borrow for us when we used all he had. If I told him he looked like a girl, he would refuse to help us.

We used the bare, blank spaces in my history workbook and the reverse side of class assignments for our drawing and story-writing. When we had exhausted all other resources, we borrowed from the teacher.

Every time Dad came home, I had to ask him for money to buy more paper.

"Good diddlely damn! Seely, what do you do with all the paper you buy? Supply the whole school? Damn it, you got a big yellow Golden Rod tablet the last time I was home!"

He'd swear, then he would give me the dime I needed to buy more paper.

Dad never stinted when it came to buying school books and supplies. He said an education was better than owning your own piece of ground. That was one thing nobody could take away from you, once you had it.

132

Doris and I would walk to Bud Watson's general store and buy the thickest pad of paper he had.

"Seely, maybe we should have chosen a trade where the training didn't cost so much," Doris said.

But we continued to waste our paper, week after week.

chapter sixteen

*F*rieda and I were
coming back from Old Man Bishop's well, the buckets
bumping our legs and slopping over into our shoes with
every step. We hadn't said a word since we lifted the
heavy buckets and started down the road to the schoolhouse.

"A penny for your thoughts, Seely."

I said, "Show me first your penny."

We laughed and set the buckets down to rest and
rubbed the red marks where the wire bucket bails had
cut dents in the palms of our hands. Then we stuck our
hands inside our coat sleeves to warm them.

"It's my birthday. I'm twelve years old today."

"My little water-bucket buddy is growing up. Pretty
soon, you'll think you're too big to carry water with old
Frieda."

She smiled and the tuck in her upper lip pulled the smile to one side of her face. "I'm too big now, Seely. I'm almost eighteen. If I didn't have my heart set on getting a school diploma, I'd quit and go to Kentucky and marry Clarence."

Clarence Bridgeman had quit school soon after the term had begun in the fall and joined the regular army. I knew Frieda had been writing to him, but I didn't think she liked him well enough to marry him. I didn't know how anyone could like him that much.

I said, "Do you really like him that much? Pretty as you are, Frieda, you could marry anybody you wanted to. Why do you want to marry Clarence?"

"After awhile, a body gives up expecting anything better, and they settle for what they can get." She gave me another crooked smile. "And I can get Clarence. He don't mind that I can't speak plain for spluttering."

I laughed with her and picked up the bucket and went on down the lane to the schoolhouse. She didn't say anything more about marriage or her leaving school. I hoped she would forget about both and let everything stay just the way it was now.

But the next day, as soon as the schoolhouse door closed behind us, Frieda started talking about Clarence.

"I feel like a fool every time I get up to leave the room," she said. "When Clarence was here, I didn't feel so bad about being so big and still in school. He was older than me, and we'd been here together since the second grade. You know what, Seely? I think the teacher picked on Clarence just to get rid of him."

I said I didn't know if the teacher picked on him or if Clarence baited the teacher just to rile him. But they sure didn't get along very well.

The last day Clarence had been to school, he and the teacher had been at odds about one thing or another from the minute the bell rang. We had been in the middle of our Health and Hygiene class when Mr. Thompson asked Clarence to tell him what a hangnail was.

Clarence had snickered and said, "Ain't that something you hang your coat on, teacher?" Then he laughed out loud.

The teacher's face was as red as a beet and the veins stood out on his neck like fat fishing worms. I thought he was going to bust a blood vessel, he was so angry. He screamed at Clarence and threw the health book with all his might and hit him between the shoulder blades. Clarence stumbled when the book struck him and nearly fell, but he caught himself just in time and slouched on down the aisle to his seat.

Mr. Thompson continued to yell at Clarence. He told him to get out and never come back. "Take your stuff with you. I want no excuse to ever see you here again," he said.

Clarence cleaned the junk from his desk and shuffled out the door, shoulders bent and shamefaced. His hair had grown long and shaggy again, and red curls fell over his ears and turned up around his collar. I could feel his hurt and shame, and I was sorry for Clarence.

Clarence never looked back, and we never saw him again.

Later on, Frieda got a letter from him. He had joined the army and was somewhere in Kentucky.

Frieda was still talking about him. "His dad went all the way to Kentucky on a Greyhound bus to see him. And once he got there, he just stayed. That's what I'd like to do," she said. "Right now, I've got a big hankering to walk to the hard road, catch one of them big buses, and keep right on going."

Frieda was still at school when we drew names for the Christmas gift exchange. I got her name and wondered all the way home what I could give her. There wasn't anything at Bud Watson's store good enough for her.

I wondered who had my name. I had a horror of going to school on the day when the Christmas gifts were given out. Maybe I'd be left out. It happened nearly every year. When the presents were all gone from under the tree, there was usually one person whose name hadn't been called. The other kids would clutch their presents close to their chests and stare wide-eyed at the one who didn't get anything. I couldn't bear to think of that ever happening to me.

Mom gave me a string of red beads that she'd had for a long time to give Frieda for Christmas. She said they were far better than anything we could buy. After we had polished the beads and put them in a box, they looked almost brand new.

The gifts at school were given out on Friday before Christmas. Frieda liked the red beads and smiled as she fastened them around her neck so everyone could see her present. Carney Collier had my name, and I wouldn't show my gift or thank him for it. He had given me a bare naked celluloid doll in a brown paper sack and tied it with a twine string. But for once, no one was left out, and Mr. Thompson gave us each one a bag of candy and an orange.

A thump-pause, thump-pause woke me on Christmas morning. When I couldn't stand the uncertainty of waiting for the next thud, I got up, dressed hurriedly in the cold room, and ran downstairs. As I pushed the door open, a blunt-pointed arrow thudded into the attic door behind me. Robert was playing with a long wooden crossbow gun. A rawhide string was pulled tight from each end of the bow and hooked over the hammer of the gun. Just as I reached the foot of the steps, Robert pulled the trigger again.

"Where did you get that thing?" I screamed at him. "You might have killed me!" I started toward him, and he began to yell for Mom.

"Mommy! Mommy!" I mocked him, and stuck out my tongue at him.

Mom came in from the kitchen, and I asked, "Who armed that little bandit?"

"Now, Seely, don't start a fuss. Rob made that and brought it for him last night."

So that was why the attic door was closed this morning. Dad was home. While he was away, our door swung wide open, and Mom left the one to her room ajar, in case we needed her during the night. Also, it allowed a little bit of heat from the stove in the front room to filter up the steps and spread through the bitter cold of the attic. Dad liked to keep all the rooms closed off and save on fuel. We were surrounded by forests and fallen trees, but he wouldn't hear of wasting a stick of stove wood to heat the attic.

It was just before Christmas that Ben Collier had told Jamie he would give him a quarter if he would haul away all the short ends and scrap lumber that were piled in a heap near the big circle-saw. Jamie and Ben shook hands on the deal, and Jamie ran home to get a bushel basket from the barn to carry the wood. I followed him back to the mill.

Floyd Perry helped us fill the basket, placing the pieces snugly to the top then running a broken slat through the wire handles so I could help Jamie carry it. We toted enough wood to fill the box behind Mom's cookstove and still the pile loomed high beside Ben's circle-saw. For three days we lugged the loaded basket home from the mill and racked the wood outside the back door.

Mom had questioned our right to the wood, but Jamie told her that Ben Collier was paying him to haul it off. Ben wanted the wood moved away from the mill, so we moved it to our house.

On the fourth evening, Ben handed Jamie a quarter and thanked him for cleaning away the scrap wood. As we hurried along the path to get home before dark, I puzzled over Jamie's good luck. It seemed to me there had to be something wrong. I knew it wasn't stealing, but I couldn't quite figure out how it was possible for us to profit twice from the same piece of work. It seemed almost dishonest.

Now, on Christmas morning, Jamie sat perched on the

step stool seemingly unaware of my shouting at Robert, eating an orange and dropping the seeds and peels on to the floor by his bare feet. He had a new navy blue sweater pulled on over his faded pajama pants, and a navy stocking cap rolled to fit the back of his head. His dark tangled curls fell from beneath the cap and over his ears, making him look like one of the paper angels that dangled from the tree beside him. He smiled at me, and orange juice dribbled from the corner of his mouth.

I said, "Jamie, you're making a mess!" And wiped his chin.

I looked around the room, but I didn't see anything for me or Julie. Maybe Mom and Dad thought we were too old for Christmas. Or it could be that Dad just didn't like us anymore and hadn't brought us a gift. He didn't act like he knew we were on the place. Maybe he had forgotten we were.

I had asked Frieda one time if she knew why it was we never got to sit on our dad's lap or get hugged like the little kids.

She'd said, "I don't think anybody likes big kids. They don't pay no attention to you after you're old enough to go to school."

"Then why do people have babies if they don't like kids?"

"Oh, they like babies all right," Frieda answered. "It's just us big kids they can't stand."

Every thought and feeling I ever had reflected plain as a mirror on my face. The hurt and disappointment I felt at being left out on Christmas must have shown truly and clearly for Mom to see.

"Rob brought something for you girls, too. Surely you don't think your daddy would bring presents for one and not the other."

By this time, I didn't know what to think of my dad. After the way he had acted during the summer and last fall, I wouldn't put anything past him.

"There's something for each of you under the tree."

I knelt to reach the largest box, and Mom stopped me.

"Seely, the red box is for you. That one wrapped in hollyberry paper is for Julie."

I grabbed my package and ran upstairs to show Julie and tell her she had a Christmas present, too.

She sat on the edge of our bed, dressed and shivering, her arms hugging herself to keep warm.

"Come on," I urged her. "There's another box bigger than mine for you to open."

She smiled and reached for my present. "First, let's see what you've got here. Then we'll go look at mine."

I ripped at the box. Torn paper and string lay unnoticed where it fell. I could feel my heart hammering as we pulled away the top layer of paper, and I saw the creamy buff and cocoa sweater lying in the box. I couldn't believe it was for me. Julie slipped the sweater around my shoulders and framed my face with the wide shawl collar.

I hoped with all my heart that Julie's gift would be as beautiful as mine. If it wasn't, I would give my Christmas sweater to her, and I would wear my old one.

Mom called us to breakfast. Julie held back, then reluctantly followed me down to the kitchen. She nearly balked when she saw Dad seated like God at the head of the table, but then she stepped quietly into the room and took her seat.

Robert had brought the crossbow to the table and laid it by his place. It took up one whole end and threatened to knock the dishes off the table every time he touched it.

I said, "Mom, does he have to bring that contraption to breakfast? I don't have room to eat!"

Julie took the gun in her hands and examined it closely. "It's no wonder Robert is so proud of this gun," she said softly. "This is the most beautiful thing I've ever seen."

She put the crossbow down carefully beside his plate and hugged him to her. "Take good care of it, honey. There's an awful lot of somebody's time and patience tied up in that."

Dad cleared his throat a couple of times, then he said, "The nights can get to be almighty long when you're away from your home and family. It's then a man has time on his hands and a chance to do some whittling, if he can lay claim to a piece of wood. Finding the right-sized piece of hickory to whittle on held me up there for awhile."

A smile played tag from his eyes to the corner of his mouth, and he chuckled deep inside to give us to understand he was joking with us. When we didn't laugh or say anything, his big rough hands moved to his coffee cup and played a soft tap, tap, tap, with the spoon on his saucer.

"I've hankered for one of them crossbows ever since I was a boy no higher than my daddy's belt buckle, like

Robert there. But my daddy never had the time given to him to make me one. During the long evenings, I got to thinking about that. Him working from daylight to dark every day of his life and no time left to call his own." Dad paused and rubbed his eyes.

"I had the time and a boy who had never heard tell of a crossbow gun and wouldn't know one if he seen it. I made up my mind then, by God, I'd make him one if it took me the rest of my life to do it. Well, it didn't take quite that long, and when it was done, I told your mother if Robert don't want it I'll keep it for myself."

The boys roared with laughter at the idea of a man Dad's size, who had to duck his head to go through doorways, playing with a toy gun.

I studied Dad's face as he laughed and joked with the boys. It was hard for me to believe he had ever been a boy. I couldn't picture him wishing for things he couldn't have, wanting them so much he could still remember what it had been like not to get them. I looked from Dad's face to Robert's and I could see the same dark-honey hair, serious blue eyes, and the sober expression as they passed the crossbow back and forth between them. I thought to myself, "Robert is the living image of Dad. It's no wonder he loves him best."

Julie looked across the table at Mom, and when their eyes met, Mom nodded and Julie glanced quickly away. She slipped quietly from the room and returned shortly carrying the holly-wrapped package.

Dad and the boys weren't paying any attention to her or to what she was doing. They didn't seem to see the box or hear the rustling paper as Julie opened it. Robert and Jamie were begging Dad to tell them how he had made the crossbow. What part did he make first? How did he get the bow to curve like a half moon? And where did he get wooden nails? They said they had never seen wooden nails before.

Dad said he made the wooden pegs, too. Then he laughed aloud at their big-eyed look of disbelief. From her place at the table, Julie gave a smothered gasp, and half-laughing, half-crying, she lifted a cloud of pale blue wool and buried her face in its softness.

When she raised her head, her eyes were wet and shining as bright as the first star over Bethlehem. She seemed to glow with the joy and wonder of her Christmas gift; more like a little girl of seven, than a grown-up seventeen.

Dad didn't see the look of love and happiness on her face as she turned toward him, started to speak, then burst out crying. For just a moment she seemed rooted to the spot, then she hugged the soft blue wool to her chest and ran from the room.

Dad seemed stunned. He spoke quietly, disbelieving. "I thought she would like it."

He turned to Mom. "Zel?"

"She liked it fine, Rob. You don't understand. . . ."

Dad shoved his chair back and got to his feet. "I'll be damned," he said. "I'll never understand that girl, Zel. Not if I live to be a hundred years old."

He closed the kitchen door gently behind him and walked into the snow flurries, bareheaded and in his shirt sleeves. Mom clucked her tongue on the roof of her mouth, shook her head, and swore he would catch his death of cold, but she made no move to take him a coat or interrupt his walk in any way.

But Julie did. She came back to the kitchen, soon after he left it, wearing her new blue sweater. When she saw Dad walking in the snow, she grabbed his old sheepskin coat off the back of the door and carried it out to him. I don't know what Dad and Julie talked about while they walked in the snow, but when they came back to the house, they were both smiling.

chapter seventeen

When we started back to school, it was fifteen degrees. The snow squeaked under our feet. It seemed like the cold stillness of January would never end.

But it did. After the first week of February, the weather turned off warm and stayed warm, more like spring than a lull in winter. The days were getting longer, and we didn't have to hurry to get home before dark. Jamie went by the sawmill on his way home from school, and Doris and I dawdled along the path to her house and played under the bare sugar maple trees. In some of them, the little spouts were still plugged in for maple sugar sap, and rusty tin cups dangled on wire hooks from the last running.

The late winter sun slanted through the tree tops,

shedding a pale yellow light around us and making weird patterns at our feet.

Doris said, "I'm glad it's daylight. Shadows like that would scare me if it was dark."

I laughed at her. "If it was dark, you couldn't see the shadows."

"Well, I could if the moon was shining!"

I said, "Doris, you're just a fraidycat. Scared of your own shadow." •

Under one of the huge maples, where the roots had broken through the soft dirt and lay on top of the ground like long, knobby-knuckled fingers, the earth was scuffed and marred by large boot tracks. It looked as if a big man had paced restlessly back and forth under the tree while he waited for someone to meet him. Near the edge of the path in the soft black dirt, we saw a smaller footprint, a woman's shoe mark. The two sets of tracks left the tree close together and faded on the hard-packed trail.

Doris stepped into the woman's tracks and pressed first one foot and then the other down on them erasing all trace but her own from under the tree.

She said, "They could have belonged to anyone. But people know we come by here. They won't think anything of it if they see our tracks along the path."

When I got home, Mom had the doors wide open and the windows raised as far as they would go, while she cleaned the copper pans with ammonia and scrubbed the pine floors with lye water. She said it was too hot. It wasn't natural.

"This weather won't last. It's too early. Probably leading up to a tornado or cyclone before it breaks, and then we'll be swamped by another spring flood," she said.

We wore our coats to school and let them drag on the path behind us on our way home. I stayed and played with Doris every evening until her mama came and warned me it was nearly dark, and I would have to go home.

Late one evening as I was loping along with my eyes on the path, I nearly ran headlong into Della and Simmy Walters walking on the path just ahead of me. Della was so thin and tiny, Simmy's arm reached all the way around her waist, and her head barely touched his shoulder. They were talking so earnestly, they hadn't heard me come up behind them. I stepped off the path and waited under the trees until they turned down the lane leading to the sawmill.

I thought to myself, "Old Simmy ain't no coward. He's walking right into Ben's reach, and Della is the only thing he has in his hands."

Doris always had a funny look on her face and drew away whenever Della's name was mentioned, so I didn't tell her I had seen Della and Simmy walking together in the woods.

Saturday morning Mom moved the furniture back against the wall and took the carpet up and carried it to the clothesline to beat the red clay dust out of it. Mom was airing bedclothes on one side of the house and beating dust from the carpet on the line in the barnyard when Doris got to our house that morning.

Doris said her mama had sent her to my house to play,

so she could get some housecleaning done. I said if we stayed around where Mom could find us, she was sure to find something for us to do. We'd probably be called to hold the line steady while Mom and Julie beat dust out of the rug into our faces.

We walked over to the Brents' house and talked to Clara. I think having Doris with me hampered Clara's overflow of information and put a damper on her questions. Usually, she just opened her mouth and let the words roll off her tongue freely. But this morning she would start to say something, then stop in the middle and change the subject.

I wondered where she came by all her news. Clara never seemed to know anything good about anybody. She carried bad news like a disease that was catching and passed it on to whoever happened to pass by.

About noon, Clara gave us peanut butter and jelly on yeast bread and told us we would have to carry it with us. She and George were leaving, going into town to do some trading.

We dragged our feet and munched the hard brown crust on the bread. When we came to the lane leading to the Walters' house, Doris said, "Let's go to Frieda's. It's too early to go home. The cleaning won't be half done yet."

At Frieda's house we looked through the Sears Roebuck catalog. Frieda showed us the red dress she had picked out for Graduation Day, if she passed. Doris and I chose the one we wanted, just alike, and knew all the time we wouldn't get it. Not in a million years!

Doris was supposed to meet her papa at the mill and walk home with him. He shut the mill down early on Saturday so the men could get to the store to do their trading. We had plenty of time to get there, so we crossed the ridge and followed the deep hollow up to the mill.

Floyd Perry saw us and motioned us back away from the buzz saw. We wandered around a bit, then found a bench and sat down to wait. While we were waiting for Ben to quit work, Doris sketched the mill and the old shed on the hillside behind it. I watched the men run the big logs past the speeding saw and stack the boards as they came off the other end like freshly sliced bread. Sawdust scattered through the air like ground cornmeal and settled like snow on the men's heads and clothes. Even their faces were covered with the fine tan dust.

I caught a glimpse of Ben sauntering over toward the big circle-saw, carrying a brand new toolbox. I wondered what he had done with the old one after he had dumped the tools out on the kitchen table that time. I don't know why it should, but the sight of Ben with a new toolbox made me think of the night I had stayed overnight with Doris. Somehow, there seemed to be some relation between the old toolbox, the screaming owls, and Della's talked-about baby.

I guess I was thinking out loud again when I said, "I wish you would draw a picture of Della's baby so I could see it. Everybody talks about Della and her baby, but I've never seen it."

I could hear the words echoing through my head and

hanging in the air between us. I wanted to call them back, swallow them, but they were already out and there was nothing I could do about it.

Doris stared at me as if I had hit her. Tears filled her eyes. She jumped up and started to run away, but then she stopped and walked slowly back to face me.

"You know Della doesn't have a baby! She and Simmy Walters got married last week, and maybe she'll have a baby, sometime. But she ain't got one now!"

Her voice rose, "You're just like everyone else, and I hate you!" As she finished speaking, tears streamed down her face, and she ran away from me to hide in the old shack on the hillside.

I didn't try to stop her. I sat on the bench and watched her go. I didn't know what to do. Mom had said if I wasn't careful, one of these days my mouth was going to get me in trouble for talking without thinking. Just this morning, when I told her I was going to Clara's, she said, "Seely, you've been around that woman so much you're getting to be just like her. I'll swear Clara's tongue is tied in the middle and flaps loose on both ends."

I guess she was right about it. Only Clara's loose tongue gave other people trouble, and mine made trouble for me. I wished I had bitten the hateful thing in two before it had hurt Doris.

I saw Ben Collier looking at me, so I got up and started to mosey along toward home. I wanted to go to the shack and tell Doris I was sorry. But I didn't think it was the time to say anything. Sometimes it's best not to say a word when a person is crying hurt.

151

I moped around the house until after supper.

"What's bothering Seely?" Mom asked Julie. "Is she sick? It's about time, I reckon."

I thought, "For Pete's sake! Can't I even think without being sick? And what does she mean, 'It's about time'? Don't tell me that now I even have to have a time to be sick!"

I slammed the door behind me and left the dishes wet and draining, to be dried later.

I met Doris just after I had crossed the footlog on Lick Crick. I was going to her house, she was coming to mine. We ran into each other's arms. She was crying, and I said over and over, "I'm sorry, Doris, I'm sorry."

She sat on the edge of the footlog, sobbed a couple of times, and wiped her nose on her loose shirttail.

"It's dirty, already," she said.

I sat down beside her and dangled my feet over the water. "Mom said I wasn't to come to your house, but I was coming anyway. She didn't say I couldn't play with you and be best friends."

She put her hand on my arm, then quickly took it away. "Maybe you won't want to be best friends when you hear what Mama said. She says no one wants to neighbor with a family whose girl has got in trouble and had a baby before she was married. Even if the baby died and the girl didn't show her face out of the house till the day she got married, they still won't let her forget it."

We sat quietly in the dark, swinging our legs over Lick Crick. Across the night sky, lightning flashed briefly, but it was too far away for us to hear the thunder.

The only sounds were the frogs singing and diving into the water from the creek bank. Far off in the night, we heard a hoot owl calling to his mate, and another owl answering him from the woods behind us.

"It wasn't a hoot owl we heard screaming the night you stayed with me. It was Della. Today at the mill, I thought you knew it was her."

I shook my head. No, I didn't know it. In the darkness, I answered her silently.

"Della's baby was dead when Mama went in to her. She called Papa and they fixed up his old tool chest with a piece of blanket to bury the baby. Mama said a girl knows when she is ready to grow up and leave home. She should have let Della marry Simmy Walters when she wanted to, then none of this would have happened."

"How do you know all this happened? You were in bed with me that night. I didn't know about it."

"I asked Mama when I got home today. I told her that people were talking about it. They thought we had a baby hidden away in our house. She said, 'No, not in the house, buried out in the apple orchard. Then she commenced to cry. She said it wasn't anybody's business. Let them say what they would. If folks didn't have somebody to talk about, they'd be sick."

I said, "Mom thought I was sick. She said it was about time."

Doris laughed softly. "Don't it beat all how nosey a girl's mama gets when it comes that time?"

"What time are you talking about now?"

"Hasn't your mama told you? Pretty soon now, every month for the rest of our lives, I guess, we'll have periods of bleeding. All girls have them. If we don't, we'll have a baby."

Well, for Pete's sake! Wasn't there anything good to look forward to when we grew up? This was the most revolting thing I had heard of yet.

I said, "I won't grow up then. I didn't want to be a girl in the first place, and I certainly don't want that to happen to me."

I could hear Mom calling, "Seely. Seely, come here this minute. Se-e-ely, you hear me!"

We sat and listened to the echoes of her voice die away. Doris took my hand and held it palm first to her face. "It will happen whether you want it to or not, Seely. You've got to grow up sometime. We can't stay children all our lives, you know that."

Lightning flashed a jagged streak across the sky, and we could hear the thunder now, rumbling through the hills and hollows.

"Doris, I've got to go in, now. Want to go with me? There's a storm coming up. Jamie and I will walk you home later."

"No, I'm not afraid anymore," she said, and then she hurriedly added, "nothing can happen so bad you can't live over it or forget it happened. Della says they can kill you, but they can't eat you. It's against the law!"

I knew that in spite of what she said, Doris was still afraid in the woods at night.

"Wait, Doris, wait for Jamie. He'll take you home." We touched hands and I started running toward the house.

chapter eighteen

*L*ong spikes of lightning split the sky and thunder rumbled and growled like an empty stomach. With every streak of lightning, the thunder reverberated through the hills, shook the house, and rattled the dishes in the corner cabinet. The storm clouds were black and rolling. The high whistling wind kept them moving on a level with the treetops like giant kites on a short string, hulking and hovering in the dark sky.

Mom was polishing the glass lamp globes with newspaper while I put the supper dishes away. We were both making more noise than necessary, trying to drown out the sounds of the approaching storm.

"Jamie should have been back from walking Doris home by now," I said. "He'll be caught in the dark woods when the storm hits, and he's scared to death of thunder storms."

"The rain is a long way off yet," Mom answered. "He'll be home and in bed long before it hits here."

But immediately following her words, making them a lie and taking away their small comfort, we were blinded by a fiery flash of light and shaken by the loud clap of thunder that came with it. Rain pounded its fists on the tin roof and beat against the windows. Mom had put Robert to bed and he'd gone to sleep. I thought the sound of the rain would surely wake him, but he slept right through it. Once I said to Mom that I hoped Floyd and Julie had made it to Nancy Ann's house before the rain started. She said there was no reason to worry about them and cupped her hands around her eyes to peer through the rain-swept glass, striving for the sight of Jamie coming home.

We had a regular gully-washer. The rain overflowed the eaves' trough and poured down the water spouts, splashing into the rain barrels and running over in a stream. Mom paced the floor from one window to the other, trying to see through the blowing rain.

At last, she said, "Lands' sakes, Seely, go to bed. You give me the shivers, sitting there with your big eyes staring at nothing."

"I'm not doing anything. I'm just waiting for Jamie."

She touched my hair as she walked by me. "I know," she said gently. "Go to bed now. Jamie probably stayed over at the Colliers'. If he'd started home and got caught in the storm, he would stop at the Walters'. He wouldn't try to come on home through a storm like this one."

I sat in the dark by the upstairs window watching the storm. When the lightning flashed, I could see the trees bent double like giants with the bellyache. For the first time in my life I wished Dad was home. He should be here. He would go right out in this storm and find Jamie and bring him home.

Once Dad had walked all over the county, stopping at every house looking for Julie and me. We had gone to Nancy Ann's house without telling anyone where we were going. We had stayed there until dark, and then we had been afraid to walk home through the woods. When night came and we weren't home, Mom grew frantic. She was sure we had been carried away by the gypsies. Dad said the gypsies weren't that damn desperate for girls, but he'd go look for us.

It had been about ten o'clock that night and sprinkling rain when Dad knocked on the Arthurs' back door. "Tell my girls to get their things. I've come to take them home."

He had switched our legs when our steps lagged, and with every swish of the willow stick, he told us what a damn fool he had made of himself hunting all over the damn county for two half-wit girls, who didn't have the sense to come home by themselves.

Dad had switched us good, but he had brought us home. If he were here now, he would go out and bring Jamie home, too.

I awoke in the morning, cold and cramped, on the floor by the window. The storm had blown itself out, and water stood ankle deep where last summer's garden had been.

White River would be out of its banks and the bottom land flooded with back water. Lick Crick would be running wild and bank full, the footlog slick or underwater, so we couldn't use it to cut through the woods. I thought the rivers were a beautiful sight to see, until they became flooded and overran their banks. Then I was afraid of them. Mom said they were a dangerous nuisance to everyone living in the hills and hollows, and something ought to be done about them. She never said what could be done, but like everything else in Greene County, she hated them.

When I went downstairs, Mom was drinking coffee at the kitchen table. She didn't look like she had been to bed all night. Her eyes, brown like Jamie's, were dull now, and her eyelids red and swollen.

She said, "I wish your daddy was here. One of us should go bring Jamie home. A body tends to forget he's just a little boy. Ten years old ain't grown up yet, not by a long sight."

"I'll go. You stay here with Robert. He'd have a conniption fit if he woke up and you weren't here."

I dodged the puddles in the gravel road, then waded into mud over my shoetops to get to the Walters' place.

Mr. Walters said they hadn't seen Jamie last night or this morning and offered to go to the Collier place for me.

I said, "No. I have to go for Jamie. I told Mom I'd bring him home."

I took the path through the woods and over the rain-slick ridge to the Collier house. I was almost there when I met Ben on his way to the sawmill.

He said, "Hey, what are you doing out so early on a day like this? I wouldn't have stepped a foot out of the house, but I wanted to see if last night's windstorm had left any of my mill standing."

"I'm on my way to your house to walk home with Jamie. I didn't have anything else to do."

Ben looked puzzled and scratched his head under his hat. He didn't look at me when he said, "The boy Jamie left our place right after he brought Doris home last night. Said he wanted to get home before the storm broke."

He hesitated a moment. "Guess he didn't make it, hey?"

"No. He didn't," I answered, and turned back toward home.

I figured Jamie would have been in a hurry and taken the shortest way home. I cut through the woods, following the path he would have taken after he had left Doris at her house. I spread the bare sucker limbs spaced like a picket fence around the tree-stump playhouses and looked inside. I stopped beneath the hanging cliff rock where we had watched the ground squirrels and chipmunks at play to see if he was there. It was warm and dry under the rock, but there was not one sign of Jamie. I searched every place where he could have found shelter from the storm until I came to the footlog on Lick Crick.

The footlog had been under water, but the creek had gone down, leaving the log wet and slick under my feet. Carefully testing each step, I crossed over Lick Crick and followed the path to the barn.

Mom was in the barn looking for Jamie. "I thought he

might have made it this far and took shelter in the hay-loft." She spoke wearily, as if the watching and waiting had worn her out.

I had been so sure he was on the path just ahead of me and I would find him safe and sound when I got home.

Mom said, "George went up the hollow toward the sawmill. He said he'd get the men to help him look for Jamie. I can't for the life of me figure where that boy can be."

She shook her head and started toward the house. I turned back to the woods and the path to the footlog. He wouldn't have tried to cross the creek above the foot-log. There was no fit place to ford the creek up that way. I thought maybe he had slipped on the wet makeshift bridge and fallen into the water. If he was hurt, I would find him down crick from the footlog. I turned my mud-caked feet downstream, my eyes never leaving the creek bank, searching for some sign that Jamie had come this way.

The river was still swift and rolling, but the flood-water had gone down until Lick Crick was about to its usual size. I marveled that in just one day I had seen Lick Crick change from a roaring, thundering river, which had threatened to ruin everything in its path, to a swift, swollen stream. "By this time tomorrow," I thought, "all the backwater will be drained into White River, and it will be as if we had never had a flood down here."

I had not found one trace of Jamie along the creek banks. I scraped the mud off my shoes and sat down to rest under the willow tree that had shaded our swimming hole in summer. I tried to think of some other place where he might have gone to get out of the storm. Ben, George, and Floyd Perry were searching the gullies and hollows back in the hills. There seemed to be no place left for me to hunt for Jamie.

A piece of dark blue cloth lapping in the waves of muddy water at the base of the tree caught my eye. Hanging onto the tree with one hand, I slid down the bank and grasped the piece of overall jacket with the other hand. The blue jacket was snagged in the river and I couldn't budge it. I pulled and tugged, and with the next hard tug the sleeve fell free, leaving a bare arm floating just beneath the surface of the murky water.

I knew then my search for Jamie was over. He was caught and held tight in the roots of our willow tree.

My hands were frozen on the soggy jacket. I couldn't drag Jamie from the muddy waves that tugged and pulled at him, but I wouldn't turn him loose. I knew I had to hold on to this last part of Jamie. I couldn't let it go free.

Ben Collier found me crouched on the creek bank and dragged me from the water's edge. I couldn't speak to him. I knew Jamie was dead, but if I didn't say it out loud, it wouldn't be true. I told myself he was playing. He would be home for supper and sleep in his bed tonight as usual.

But I couldn't tell myself it wasn't my fault. I knew I was to blame. If I had gone with him, this would never have happened. I knew he was afraid of the dark woods and thunderstorms, but I had sent him out alone, anyway. I had urged him to go.

"Hurry, Jamie," I told him. "Run to the woods. Doris is waiting for you."

If I had done as Mom had told me, Jamie would be alive. How many times had Mom said to me, "Seely, stay with Jamie and look after him." Or she would caution me, "Seely, take care of your brother."

But instead of blaming me, Mom tried to comfort me. "You have to understand, Seely. It wasn't anyone's fault."

She took my hands and pulled me close to her. "He had one of his spells and fell into the flood water. A sudden flash of lightning or just the noise of the storm could have brought it on him. We never knew what caused those spells. But we do know Jamie never suffered. He never once complained of any pain after he woke up."

"I promised I'd care for him." I sobbed. "I said I'd help, but I wasn't there to help him."

"Hush now, you've always cared for Jamie. Ever since you were knee-high to a grasshopper, you two were together. We couldn't separate you."

I guess she must have realized we were separated now. She wiped my face on her aprontail and took me on her lap as if I was a baby. She rocked back and forth, patting and soothing me as she spoke. "I won't have you blaming yourself for something that couldn't be helped. I've made up my mind, there'll be no more laying the blame on anyone in this family." She spoke so softly, I could barely hear her words. "I have faulted your daddy every day for moving us to these godforsaken hills. I've hardly given him a kind word from the first minute I set foot on this place. It's no wonder he's been so harsh and unkind at times. There were few times that I can recall any kindness to him."

She rocked quietly for a moment, the soft creak of the rockers lulling me. "Once I felt I could never forgive him for it, but there has been too much bitterness and unforgiving around here. Now, we'll not use Jamie's death as a base for building more misery."

Clara Brent came and carried the marble-topped stand table home with her. To make room for the coffin, I supposed. Mom helped her carry the table out to the car. While they were tucking spread rugs to protect the finish, Mom said, "I do appreciate this, Clara. It's real kind of you. I'd always pictured Grandma's table staying in the family, but I reckon she'd understand if she knew why I'm parting with it."

Clara's face seemed to crumble and cave in. She turned away and busied herself with the rugs. After awhile she touched Mom's arm and said, "George and me are glad to do whatever we can, Zel."

Neighbors who had never been in our house came out of the hills and hollows to bring baskets of cooked food and track mud into the front room. They stood awkwardly ill at ease and stared at Jamie. Mom cried and Dad shook hands silently. I ran and hid in the storeroom under the stairs. Julie fixed meals, which no one felt like eating, and took care of Robert, while I wandered around like a lost soul or sat quietly in the dark storeroom, away from everyone.

On the last evening, Doris and Frieda came to see Jamie. I saw them as they approached the house, walking slowly and holding hands as if drawing courage from each other to come inside.

From my hiding place, I heard Mom call my name. Then she said, "I don't know where that girl gets to. She was here a moment ago."

I heard their steps falter as they tiptoed to the place where Jamie lay. There was a long silence, then the front door closed gently behind them. The sound of their running feet as they fled our house was the last thing I heard. I fell asleep and slept all night in the dark space under the stair steps.

At the funeral, I couldn't look at Jamie. I didn't like it, and I knew he wouldn't like it, either. They had dressed him in stiff new corduroy pants with a jacket to match and folded his arms across his chest. He looked so uncomfortable, dressed up with his shoes on, lying on the puckered white satin pillows. I thought, "God must feel the same way about little boys that Dad said Mom did about little new potatoes; He just couldn't keep His hands off and let Jamie grow up."

Someone had borrowed two saw horses from Ben Collier's mill and set the wooden box across them. And now Jamie lay before the altar rail like a holy sacrifice for all the people who had come to hear Mom's sobbing and touch Dad's hand.

I sat beside Julie and counted the homemade bunches of flowers placed near the coffin. The women had made them by cutting tin cans into narrow strips and tying red and white crepe paper flowers to the metal stems. There were nine tin can baskets and three crepe paper flowers to each stem. I guess they couldn't find any green paper, there wasn't a leaf on any of them.

There was one store-bought bunch of fresh yellow flowers and green ferns spread across the casket. "From George and Clara," it said in wide gold letters on the ribbon.

I heard the preacher say, "Then in His mercy, may He grant you a safe lodging, and a holy rest and peace at last. Amen."

It was then I cried for Jamie. The flowers blurred into one long splash of color. I was blind to the time and the people's faces, until at last it was over, and we could return to a cold, empty house.

We left the flowers, the homemade and the store-bought ones, on the muddy red clay mound in the Flat Hollow churchyard.

chapter nineteen

*M*arch came to the hills like a wild animal, spitting snow and sleet and growling with the cold north wind that swept down the dark hollows. Doris and I huddled deep in our coats and let the strong gusts of wind push us to school. Then we walked backwards so we wouldn't have to face the bite and sting going home.

I had never been so cold. Even the red-hot potbellied stove in the front room at home failed to warm me. There didn't seem to be any warmth anywhere in the quiet house. I wondered if it was harder to heat an empty, quiet house than a noisy one filled with kids. I thought, "For a little boy, Jamie sure took up a lot of room."

Julie was gone, too. She had left home soon after the funeral and moved in with Nancy Ann and her mother.

Julie said if she stayed with them she could work after school each day and make enough money to pay for her graduation things. She said she thought Mom and Dad had enough to pay for right now. She was just trying to make things easier for us all.

She smiled at Mom and said, "I spend most of my time at Nancy's house. I might as well take my clothes and live there."

Mom had said, "Go ahead, Julie, have it your own way. But your daddy will bring you home."

But he hadn't.

I slept on my side of the attic room, and Robert slept in the bed he had shared with Jamie. At first, he had begged to sleep with me. Then it seemed as though every night he would wake me up crawling into my bed or cuddling behind me, his feet like icicles on the back of my legs.

I would chase him back to his own bed where he would curl himself around a pillow for bed company and close his eyes. When I was sure he was sleeping and not just playing possum, I would tuck the covers tight to him so he wouldn't sleep cold and go back to bed.

I knew that sometime we would get used to the empty places beside us where Julie and Jamie had always been, but it would take a lot of night time.

The long, cold winter had finally blown itself out, and now we had a warm, gentle breeze coming up from the south, bringing the smell of spring to the hills. The ice had broken loose from the river banks and had been washed downstream by the early spring rains.

167

I guess my dreams of staying a child forever had been washed away with the winter ice, because they were gone now. I had grown up during the last two months.

Mom said, "Don't worry about it, Seely. It's a natural thing. I knew it was about time, but . . ."

"If you knew, why didn't you tell me?"

I don't know where I found the courage to speak. Before I knew it, the words were out.

"Seely, if a body was told everything to expect from living, there would be no joy in their blessings. And I doubt that they'd be able to bear the trouble and sorrow if they knew about it beforehand."

I suspected that everyone could tell it just by looking at me. I searched my face in the washstand mirror for signs of a change. I thought surely there would be something different, but I was just the same as I had always been.

Other things changed during this time, but it was so bit-by-bit that I didn't notice until it had become a set pattern. It used to be Dad would get home late on Saturday night once a month, sleep while we were at church, and leave for Crowe right after Sunday dinner. But lately, he had been coming home early every Friday evening and leaving just before daylight on Monday morning.

If he and Mom weren't so old and hadn't been married for so long, I would have sworn he was courting her. He acted like it.

He followed her to the well, drew the water, then carried it back to the kitchen. On Sundays, he got up and went to church with Mom. And while she cooked dinner, he sat in the kitchen, smoked his pipe, and played checkers with Robert. Robert usually won the game because Dad was watching Mom instead of the checkerboard.

Dad seemed surprised when I brought home an eighth-grade report card for him to sign. He said I was pretty young to be thinking about high school, wasn't I? But he seemed pleased with me for once.

I found myself walking close to Dad's chair or brushing his arm in passing, wanting to share some of the attention he gave so generously to Robert. At times I wondered when I had stopped being afraid of Dad and started liking him again. I guess it must have been when he and Mom began to like each other again.

One evening after supper, Dad took out his pipe, carefully measured in the tobacco, and tamped it tight with his thumb. He fired a long splinter from the live coals in the cookstove and lit it, puffing long and hard, and sending small gray clouds to the ceiling.

When he had the pipe drawing to his liking, he looked at me and said, "Your mother will be needing a lot of help for the next week or so, packing and sorting the things she'll want to move to Lawrence County. It's a good house, big enough to stretch in, and not an hour's drive from my work. You come straight home from school and do as she tells you. We want to have things ready to go as soon as school is out for the summer."

I said, "Moving? But why . . .?"

Mom said, "Hush, and listen to your dad."

He frowned and said, "Let her speak her piece, Zel. She's getting old enough to have some say about what she does and where she's going from now on."

"There's people here," I began. "Julie and Jamie, we can't leave them. And there's others, too."

Dad puffed on his pipe and blew a smoke screen between us. "There will be people where we're going, Seely."

The smoke cleared, and I could see the deep lines around his eyes and mouth. "There ain't nothing we can do about Jamie. Not anymore. And Julie made her own choice. We don't need to worry about her. That girl has spunk and grit enough for two her size. She'll get along just fine. You'll see, when she comes home."

I listened to the tone of his voice more than the words he spoke. I thought, "Why, he's proud of Julie. He is truly proud of her!"

It was a good feeling to know he hadn't just thrown Julie away as if she didn't belong to us any longer. He hadn't tried to hold her or make her stay. He had let her go as if he didn't care. But now, he was looking forward to her homecoming.

Dad said, "Floyd Perry is a good boy. Make a fine man someday. And I'll say this for him, he ain't afraid of work. When they're married, he'll see to it that Julie never wants for a thing."

"But she ain't marrying Floyd."

"Ah, but she will. Whenever she is ready to settle down, Floyd will be there waiting for her."

Dad knocked the doddle out of his pipe and slid his

chair back from the table as if to say he would hear no more about it. The matter was closed as far as he was concerned.

I rid up the table, and Mom started washing the dishes.

"It will be a load off my mind to get out of these hills. We've had nothing but trouble and hard times down here. Jase dead by his own hand, and Dicie gone away to where none can reach her; friends I've known all my life taken by these infernal hills."

Mom dried her hands on her apron, then brushed the damp strands of hair from her face. "And Jamie, what chance of a life of any kind did he ever have down here?" She moved between the table and cabinets putting away the dishes I had wiped. "Well, times are better now, all over. There'll be no more hand-to-mouth living for you and Robert, once we're settled in this new place."

I didn't say anything. I'd had my say with Dad, and it hadn't done a lick of good.

She said, "There's nothing here for us, Seely. There never was. No future, nothing to look forward to; just these dark hollows and everlasting hills closing in and squeezing the life out of a body." She stood with her hands empty, looking out into the night. "There were times when I thought I'd lose all my children to them shadowy woods and dark hollows." She spoke quietly. "Lord knows, I've lost enough here."

I thought to myself, "There's a kind of light in the woods when you know where to look for it. They are not all shadows and darkness. If you stand back and look at the woods, you can always find a path through them.

I've roamed these hills and hollows from one end to the other, and the dark didn't get me."

Pretty soon now, I thought, the white dogwood blossoms would be spreading across the hills and the flowers from the redbud would mingle among them, brightening up the woods and hillsides. Streaks of warm sunshine on the floor of the forest would bring out the creamy kitten britches and the purple violets, too, but I wouldn't know when; I wouldn't be here to see them.

I rushed home every afternoon to help Mom pack and crate the things she wanted to take with her. We dragged the old barrel-topped trunk out of the storage space for Mom to pack her memory box in. The trunk used to set against the wall in the front room with Mom's yellow and white wedding ring quilt folded over its humped lid, but after she traded the quilt to Clara, she said the trunk was an ugly old thing and moved it under the attic steps and closed the door.

It was Mom's trunk to keep her treasures in, and she wouldn't allow us kids to rummage through it. But we knew all the things it held and the musty odor of age and sandalwood that escaped when we lifted the lid.

Mom's memory box held all of Jamie's things. There wasn't much. Just a few clothes, his Indian arrow heads, some bright marbles, and the old harmonica Floyd had given him. He had finally learned to play one song on it —"Oh, where, oh, where has my little dog gone? Oh, where, oh, where can he be?" and he had played it from daylight till dark.

Mom put her wedding dress with the lacy veil and the

other stuff that had been in the trunk back on top of Jamie's things and locked the lid.

By the end of the week, the house was bare of everything but what we needed to get by until school was out.

Clara brought Great-grandmother Curry's marble-topped table back to Mom and took a crate of chickens home with her in the trunk of the car. Later that same day, George came and led the cow away. He waved and called back over his shoulder, "Clara will be over in the morning for the rest of them chickens."

Mom ran her hand over the table and caressed the cool marble top. "I guess that just about takes care of everything. I'm rid of the livestock, and I've got Grandma's table back home where it belongs. Now we're all ready to go as soon as school is out."

Everything seemed to hinge on the last day of school. Everyone was ready to go but me.

I would walk through the kitchen, wander around the front room, go up to the attic, turn around, and go back to the kitchen. Sometimes, I'd roam about the yard, but never farther than the empty barn and not ever out of earshot, in case Mom needed me. Only once I ventured out of the yard. I ran to the cave and carried all our pretty junk back to the gully behind Lick Crick. I stood on the rim and pitched it away piece by piece and watched the bright amber bottles shatter into a million pieces when they hit the rocks.

I rolled my notebooks into a tight roll and tied a string around them. I didn't know what to do with them, so I kept them. I didn't want to use them. I couldn't seem to settle down in one place and be quiet long enough to write. Even when I wasn't up and about, I felt like I was racing against time.

Dad didn't seem to mind the bare floors and stacked boxes all over the house. He came home in a good humor and didn't appear to be in any great hurry to leave and go back to Crowe. It was as if a weight had been lifted from his shoulders or something he couldn't bear to face had been removed from his sight.

Where he had once found fault, he now found favor. He didn't even cuss and raise Cain when Robert left the washbasin on a chair and I sat down in it with my school dress on.

He laughed at me. "Don't fuss at him, Seely. There's no school tomorrow, and it will dry before Monday."

We only had another week of school. Doris and I would be the only ones graduating from the eighth grade. As hard as Frieda had tried and as long as she had waited to get a diploma, she had left home one day and never come back.

No one seemed to know where she had gone. I figured she had finally caught one of the big buses she talked about so much and gone to Kentucky.

Doris and I would be the last pupils to graduate from McVille grade school. The one-room schoolhouse had served its purpose in Greene County, and now it would be torn down. Next year all the kids would go by bus to the schools at the county seat.

"It's a shame it wasn't closed down last year." I told

Doris, as I slipped and skidded through the red clay mud. "If it had been, I'd be riding instead of sliding to finish this last week of school."

Every night I fussed and fumed while I cleaned the mud off my shoes. I told Mom it was like doing dishes; there was no end to it. You did it today, and tomorrow it was all to do over again.

She said, "Don't complain, Seely. Next year you won't have to wade red clay mud to get to school every day. Soon this will all be outgrown like them shoes you're cleaning."

Dad gave me the money to get a new dress for my graduation day. I went to the county seat with Clara Brent and bought three yards of orange, brown, and yellow voile to make a dress, and a pair of high-heeled slippers to wear with it. Clara said she used to be quite a hand at sewing. She would be glad to make up the piece of goods for me.

She made it up and used every scrap of the material to do it. The dress had a full gathered skirt with a wide flounce, long sleeves with ruffles at the cuffs, and high neck. I tried it on and practiced walking in the high heels, but the heels caught in the hem of the skirt and my ankles turned with every other step.

I had to learn to walk in them before Friday. I was afraid I'd trip and fall flat on my face when I wore them to get my diploma.

Mom said it wasn't proper for a twelve-year-old girl to wear spike heels, and I shouldn't have been allowed to buy them. She added that if she'd been along, the money wouldn't have been wasted on such foolishness. She thought I'd made a big mistake buying them.

Dad said, "Oh, leave her be, Zel. She'll outgrow the wonder of new high heels and early spring soon enough."

He laughed and waggled his pipe stem at me. "Mark my words, Zel. That girl will make bigger mistakes in her life than the proper kind of shoes to wear. Don't spoil it for her. Let her find that out for herself."

This was the first I knew that I could make a mistake and not be burned in hellfire and brimstone for it. I thought maybe making allowances for mistakes was one of the benefits given to grown-ups, but denied to children.

chapter twenty

On graduation day, I carried the new shoes and walked barefoot until I was in sight of the schoolhouse. Then I wiped the mud off my feet on the wet grass and put on the shoes. My feet slipped into my shoes easier wet than they had dry. The flounce caught on my shoe heel, so I held the skirt above my knees while I crossed the playground to the door.

A new dress and shoes without mud on them was enough to turn everyone's head, but I hadn't expected the way they turned to look when I stepped into the school room. It was packed to the walls with parents, children, and crying babies when I marched down the aisle between the crowded desks to the one I had claimed for the past eight months.

Snickers and giggles followed me to my seat. I felt my face flush hot and red. I wished with all my heart for the old faded lavender skirt and blouse I had worn to school all winter. No one would have noticed me in my old dress.

I scanned the faces for Doris and found her sitting across the room with her folks. She was smiling and motioning for me to come sit with her. But I shook my head and turned away.

She probably just wanted to talk about Indianapolis, I thought. That was all I had heard since the day her mama had promised her she could stay with Della and Simmy and go to high school up there.

"They have art schools in Indianapolis, and I can attend one of them if I'm eligible for enrollment."

Doris had been learning a lot of new big words and using them every chance she got. She said she didn't want her friends in Indianapolis to think she was an ignorant hillbilly.

I said, "What friends? You don't have any friends up there, yet. Besides, if they don't like you the way you are, they're not very good friends."

Her blue eyes had a devilish look when she replied, "Seely, are you insinuating I'm an ignorant hillbilly?"

We had both laughed. But I knew that was all she ever thought about.

I didn't hear the end-of-the-year program the children gave for their parents at the close of every school year. I was too busy telling myself, "You can stand anything for an hour. Just one more hour and this will all be behind you. Then no more school, no more mud to wade; and what's more important, you will have a diploma from common school."

The hour was over and Mr. Thompson was calling my name. "Caroline Cecilia Robinson!"

I sat still and quiet at my desk. I wasn't ready or eager to call attention to myself again.

"Seely," he called softly.

He held a rolled paper tied with a blue ribbon. I could see the man with the axe and oxen on the official seal of Indiana stamped on the paper. Mr. Thompson tapped the rolled diploma lightly against his hand and held it out to me.

"Like offering a carrot to a jackass," I thought, as I got to my feet.

I didn't look at the crowd. I felt as though I was walking a high, narrow footlog with Lick Crick roaring far below me. If I didn't look down, I'd be home safe; look down or hesitate, and I would be lost forever. I closed my mind to every thought but one. "It's over and I've made it! Just a few steps more. . . ."

Then my heel caught in my flounce, my ankle turned, and I stumbled the rest of the way to the raised platform.

Mr. Thompson took my hand to steady me and turned me to face the noisy, crowded room.

"I'm proud and happy to be the one to present this diploma to Cecilia Robinson. She is my first straight A student and has a perfect attendance record, also."

Mom and Dad should be getting this commendation, I thought. If they hadn't forced me into the rain and cold every day with threats of "a licking at school, two at home," I would never have done it.

Mr. Thompson said the same thing every year, but I made myself listen to the end of his prepared speech.

"With her thirst for knowledge and her determination to learn, I'm sure she won't disappoint me. Seely, this is yours. You've earned it."

I mumbled my thanks and accepted the precious piece of paper I had run the gauntlet to receive.

Everyone was clapping their hands, shouting, and stomping their feet as I fled from the room for the last time. As I crossed the worn threshold, I thought, "Someone else besides me will sweep up the dried mud and dust stomped off their heavy shoes here today."

I wasn't sure whether I was happy or sorry to see the last of this one-room schoolhouse. It was the end to a way of living that I had grown used to, and I dreaded to leave it for a new school somewhere else.

The small, unfriendly faces, which had once seemed so strange to me, were now as familiar as my own. We had shared our lunch sacks and we drank from the same tin cup. I would miss them. They were my friends.

I would have to make new friends where I was going, grown-up friends that would last awhile. And to do that, I would have to act like a grown-up. I wasn't a child, but I had a long way to go before I would be a grown-up woman. I felt as though I had passed the first barrier and hurdled the first obstacle to growing up. Now I wanted to be a woman.

Childhood had lost its appeal for me. Without Jamie,

it didn't seem so wonderful that I'd want to stay there forever. I would be leaving Jamie behind. He belonged to my childhood. And Teddy had been a part of it, too.

"But they would always be children," I thought. "Beautiful, carefree children to whom these hills had been a lovely place for a short stay." Tomorrow I'll start acting grown-up, I told myself, first thing tomorrow morning. But right now, I have to be getting home.

I kicked off the high-heeled shoes and threw them over the hill into the buckbrush. Holding my skirt above my knees, away from the mud and wet weeds, I walked home the same way I had come to school—skirt hiked above my knees and barefoot.

Two days later, I stood beside the borrowed truck and pretended I was glad we were moving out of the hills. If I hadn't been laughing and talking, I would have been wiping tears like Doris or holding my breath like Julie, to keep from crying.

Dad slid behind the steering wheel, and Mom helped Robert up into the seat beside Dad. With her hand on the cab door, she said, "Seely, you'd better tell Julie good-bye now and get on the truck. We're ready to go."

Julie was dry-eyed and quiet, but Doris unashamedly wiped tears away with her hand, leaving wet streaks on her face. For the first time, we didn't have a word to say to each other. And this would be the last chance we had to speak.

Dad started the truck and raced the motor. I climbed aboard and settled myself in a tight pocket between the rolled carpet and bedding. That cold November day when Julie, Jamie, and I had ridden to Greene County on the back of Jase Perry's old rattletrap truck seemed like a hundred years ago.

There would be no one to share the cookies or the warm sunshine on this trip out of the hills. Jamie, Julie, and Jase were staying in Greene County. Jase and Jamie would remain throughout eternity, but Julie, only for a little while. Then like the swift clear rivers, she and Floyd would move out of the hills and make their way into the world.

As the truck pulled away in high gear, I rested my knees on the rolled carpet and waved to Julie and Doris.

Doris ran after the fast moving truck, crying, "Come back, Seely! Come back! Come back!"

I ducked my head to miss the tree limbs swinging low over the road. When I raised my head and looked back, they were gone from sight.